EYE O. ... .

Book Two in the Storm Series

A NOVEL

By
M. Stratton

Eye of the Storm

For Michael, my husband.
You are my shelter, my rock, my calm when life's
storms blow around us.

ACKNOWLEDGEMENTS

To my readers, thank you so much for picking up this book and reading it. It amazes me when I hear from readers who love my stories. I cherish each and every one of you. I cannot thank you enough for taking a chance on a new author when I published After the Storm and then liking it so much you picked this one up.

To the bloggers out there. Oh my gosh, I wouldn't be where I am today without you. I have had the honor of meeting some really wonderful ladies who have taken time out of their busy schedule to talk to me, or post about my books. Thank you so very, very, very much.

To my Stratton's Stars Street Team. You are so totally awesome and I love you all. You rock my world with all of your support.

To my fellow authors. Wow! Some really fabulous people out there. I couldn't begin to list all of them that have helped me. My Indie Authors and AS101, I cannot even begin to say how much you all have helped me.

My beta reads, Carey, Chelle, Heather, Jennifer, and Kristina your love of my writing and the excitement you have for my books keeps me going.

To my editor Angi Black, thank you so much for transforming my mess into something people can actually understand when they read.

My clean readers Gloria and Tiffani, I love you both so much.

My assistant, Michele I couldn't do half the things I've been able to do without your help. I thank my lucky stars every day we met.

To my family, especially my husband who has had to pick up the slack from me spending my nights and weekends writing and marketing, thank you so much for your support and listening to me.

AFTER THE STORM

Book One in the Storm Series

NOTE FROM THE AUTHOR:
If you have not already read After the Storm please do so. I understand that might not be possible so please read the following to get an idea as to what happened and be brought up to date. The following contains spoilers from After the Storm.

Thank you,
M. Stratton

Alexia "Lexi" Hanson – Lexi moved from La Jolla, California, into her grandmother's home in Ipswich, Massachusetts, after her death. She spent her time helping out at the local senior center, Golden Ages, taking photographs, and playing with her rescue dog, Pepper. After spending considerable amount of time and energy rebuilding her new life, she thought it was complete, until her neighbor moved in for an extended vacation.

Noah Matthews – After fifteen years on the road making music and playing to sell-out crowds with the band Last Stand, Noah needed a break. His bandmates, all married with children, were spending time with their families, so Noah went to his beach house to relax and spend time with the only family he had left, Sam and Martha Edwards, the caretakers for his home and his godparents. Things change after he meets his neighbor crawling through his garden one morning.

Patsy Hanson – Grandmother to Lexi and ringleader for the Fearsome Foursome. The ladies had met when they were in college and formed an alliance that lasted through the years. For a while after Patsy died, the group didn't cause as much trouble, but after a few years the Troublesome Trio was born.

Evelyne Stone – The new ringleader of the group. Evelyne will say and do anything she pleases.

Leigh Winslow – Second in command she enjoys seeing if she can shock people by what she does and says.

Marie Holmes – Has always been the voice of reason. The most conservative of the three, but don't let that fool you, you don't want to let your guard down around her.

Evie Taylor – Lexi's best friend and Evelyne's granddaughter. The apple didn't fall far from the tree with Evie; she is very much like her grandmother. Evie and Lexi spent many summers growing up together in Ipswich and causing trouble. Evie owns a bookstore and café in Boston. She recently hired Jesse Fields as a manager to help her.

Jackson "Jack" Taylor – Evie's older brother. He has spent his life roaming the world after a football injury ended his career with the Pittsburg Steelers. While he might seem carefree, his family loyalty runs deep.

Kat Snyder – Is the bodyguard Noah hired to protect Lexi. Very quiet and reserved she doesn't share much with the others.

Anthony Maldono – Growing up he had the best things in life, loving parents and world travel. It wasn't until he was in his early twenties that things started to go wrong. Taking over the family business after his parents died didn't ease the heartache at their sudden death or the other deaths that seemed to follow him. Things took a turn for the worse when Anthony went out on a date with Lexi, soon after he was accused of raping and beating her. Being sent to prison for something he didn't do was just another event in his string of bad luck.

Jeremy Ellison – When the one woman he truly loved was stolen from him in his early twenties by Anthony Maldono he could no longer keep the monster he was hidden. Following Anthony over the years he systemically took everything he could from him. He learned everything he could about him until he became him, both mentally and physically. As his madness grew, so did his crimes. Once he got a taste for murder there was nothing that could stop him.

AFTER THE STORM
Bonus Material

Noah and Lexi's Wedding
May 25th

Lexi stood before the full length mirror looking at her reflection. Never in her wildest dreams would she ever think she'd be marrying rock-and-roll's hottest star. Smiling to herself, she remembered the first day they met in his garden, here some woman was crawling around it and he took it all in stride. They started out as friends, doing things that were normal and so important to Lexi, things Noah hadn't done in years. He'd even met the Troublesome Trio, Evelyne, Leigh and Marie, and lived to tell about it.

Then strange things started to happen. Things that shouldn't have been happening. Noah was her rock through the whole thing. While she didn't like having to depend on anyone, and made some stupid choices, everything came out fine in the end. Noah had saved her. She hoped she'd learned to lean on him more and not be so independent, but there were still times. Especially knowing that Jeremy was still out there. He could come back at any moment to take her happiness away. Then there was Anthony. He had been released months ago. She still felt bad about sending an innocent man to prison but was trying to forgive herself.

Her wedding day. Looking at the other women gathered around getting ready, in the reflection in the mirror she locked eyes with Evie, her best friend. The friend that helped her through the first attack and was there last September to help again. Kenyon, Dre and Sam sat together talking making up the last of her bridesmaids. Her mother was rushing around making sure everything was just perfect and trying not to cry. Kat stood in the background like usual, watching but never interacting.

"Hey, beautiful," Evie came up behind Lexi and wrapped her arms around her being careful not to mess up her gown. "You ready for your big day marrying the smoking hot Noah Matthews?"

"More than ready." A smile that reached her eyes spread across her face.

"So you're saying I haven't got a chance?"

"Ha-ha. Like you ever had one once he saw my ass wiggling around his garden."

"He still hasn't told you where you're going for your honeymoon?"

"Nope. The bastard. It's killing me. I have no idea what to pack."

Evie raised her eyebrows at her. "Do you really think you're going to be wearing that many clothes to begin with?"

"Well, I have to travel there and back don't I?"

"True. Are you ready?"

"I've been waiting for this day my whole life and once I met Noah everything just fell into place. I can't wait for us to begin our lives together.

~*~

Noah stood at the front of the church waiting for Lexi. His chest constricted at the thought of everything they'd gone through to get here. The Last Man Standing would be no more. He couldn't wait to make her officially his. He would have eloped if she would've allowed it, although he was surprised at how quickly it had all come together.

The Troublesome Trio were led in and they made a big show of making sure they said hello to all of the single men, no matter the age, as they made their way to the front row. He chuckled to himself about his bandmates meeting them for the first time. The ladies had the time of their lives giving them a hard time. Who'd have thought guys that were so used to women grabbing them would be running scared from three little old ladies.

He watched as the ushers brought in Sam and Martha and sat them in the typical spot for groom's parents. Closing his eyes, he wished his mother could be here today. *Mom, I did it. I'm marrying someone you would love, someone I wish you could have met. I'll do everything I can to show her everyday how much I love her and protect her.*

Someone slapping his back interrupted his thoughts. Turning he saw Ren grinning at him. "Snap out of it boy, it's almost time."

"Yeah, do we need to have the car ready so you can bolt?" Dylan smirked.

"We can have you out of here in two minutes flat," chimed in Rob.

"Asshats. I'm not going anywhere. Try to act civilized, we're in church."

"Yeah, but we aren't the ones who just swore in a church." Jackson laughed. "Good job."

"Shut up," was all Noah could think to say. He took a deep breath as the music began. *Finally.*

As the flower girls, ring bearer and bridesmaids made their way up the aisle, his eyes stayed pinned to the doorway waiting for Lexi to appear. When he finally did, all the air whooshed out of his lungs and his heart ached at her beauty. He barely registered that her father was there by her side. It took all he had not to rush to meet her. The closer she got the more everyone faded into the background. He only had eyes for her.

Shaking hands with her father he looked away from Lexi for the first time. "Sir, thank you for raising such a wonderful woman. I'll take care of her."

"Welcome to the family." Lexi's father turned and kissed her on the cheek. "I love you, baby girl."

"I love you, too, Daddy."

Noah took her hand and together, they turned toward the pastor. Time seemed to go both slow and fast. Focusing on her, he wanted to remember every moment forever. The old wood of the church lit up by the sun streaming through the stained glass windows, the smell of the candles. The people that meant the most to both of them, smiling and happy for them. Lexi, beautiful Lexi in her white wedding gown glowing with excitement walking towards him.

When it was time for their vows, Noah watched as tears pooled in her eyes. Using his thumb, he wiped them away. Finally, it was time to take her in his arms and have their first kiss as husband and wife.

Grinning as the cheers went up throughout the church, they turned and faced everyone as husband and wife. For Noah, it was better than a standing ovation at Madison Square Garden.

Evie sat down at the head table and watched her best friend dance the night away with her new husband. Everything was perfect, she stared wistfully at her friend's joy. It was a beautiful day. After everything Lexi had been through, she deserved this. Noah and his bandmates left their women on the dance floor and headed for the stage. Curious, Evie got up and walked over to Lexi and the other band wives.

"What are they up to?" Sam asked.

"With those four, only God knows." Dre replied.

Noah took the mic. "Thank you everyone for coming to share our special day. If you don't mind, the guys and I would like to play a special song for my bride."

Evie looked over at Lexi at the opening notes to George Strait's *I Cross My Heart*. There was a sentimental smile on her face as she gently rocked back and forth to the song.

Hearing the words of the song, Evie was struck by a longing to have something like that in her life. She knew what they had didn't come along every day. She had to find some way to make sure their happiness continued. Whatever it took, she would find a way to ensure the darkness never found them again.

EYE OF THE STORM
Book Two in the Storm Series

- PROLOGUE -

Anthony Maldono sat back in his chair and looked out the window of his home in La Jolla California at the ocean. The turbulent waves crashed on the beach and he felt it fit his mood exactly. He looked at the computer screen and scowled at the e-mail which was still waiting for his reply, he stood and walked over to where he kept his files his private investigators compiled for him about everyone and everything involved with Alexia Hanson and Jeremy Ellison. Looking through them until he came to the one labeled "Evie Taylor," he pulled it out and started to review it.

He didn't understand why she would contact him. Thinking it might be good to surprise her, he started moving his plans up.

~*~

Jeremy lay back in the bed, staring up at the ceiling, listening to the gossip show coming from the other room about Alexia and Noah's wedding. Right now, he hated his life. He knew it was temporary, but he couldn't wait for a change to come. A change he was going to make.

He formulated his plan. He'd spent considerable time and money keeping track of everybody while staying hidden. He knew Anthony Maldono as well as he knew himself and he knew what Anthony would do next. He wasn't done making Anthony's life miserable. Time to step it up a level.

For the past nine months he'd watched the authorities run around trying to find him and Anthony made a free man, it was time to start moving. It made his blood pump that he was finally going to be able to do something. He looked into the other room where the woman he had to depend on was shoving fist after fist of popcorn in her mouth. He wanted to get up and stick a knife in her gut. He hated her. He wanted her dead. But he had to wait since he had a plan. A plan that would increase the stakes in the game he was playing.

– CHAPTER ONE –

One month after Noah and Lexi's wedding…

Evie Taylor sighed and flopped down in the chair. She tossed the dusting rag on the table, tilted her head back and closed her eyes. She was bored and longed to get back to Boston to run her bookstore and café. The past ten months she'd spent two extended stays back home. Once for Lexi and now for her grandmother. She'd heard from Jesse and everything was running fine, but she missed new shipments coming in and setting up the displays. Not to mention, getting to sample new desserts from the café. She loved helping a fellow booklover find a new author. In fact, she set up a whole section of the book store for indie authors. It opened a whole new world to her regular customers.

She looked around her grandmother's living room. Knickknacks as far as the eye could see. But that was how bored she was; she'd resorted to dusting.

She'd come home to Ipswich, Massachusetts when her best friend, Lexi Hanson, now Matthews, had been attacked. She remembered the fear and anger that coursed through her veins when she got the phone call. The drive up was a blur, she couldn't get there fast enough. In the weeks that followed, she never left Lexi. She completely amazed her with her strength.

Now she was back in Ipswich again, taking care of her grandmother who broke her arm partying with one of the male guests in a hotel room. She shivered thinking about what they were doing that could have gotten her grandmother's arm broken. She knew it wasn't pretty since her grandmother was naked when the paramedics arrived.

"Evie honey, do you want something for lunch?" Evelyne Stone called from the kitchen.

Evie hefted herself up out of the chair, walked into the kitchen, and put her hands on her hips. "Grandma, why am I here if you insist on doing everything yourself?"

Evelyne tsked, "Now honey, you know I need you, but there are some things I can do myself. Besides I need to get my wing back in working order, sooner rather than later, we've got a girl's cruise coming up in a month and there are going to be men that need taming." She tried to wave her arm around almost knocking over the pitcher of iced tea on the counter.

Evie rushed over and caught it, giving her grandmother a look. "Can you please take it down a notch? You aren't fifty anymore."

"Pah. Come on, honey, lighten up. I know you've got it in you. Maybe you should go with us. I know there will be some young hot guys there."

"And how do you know this?"

"Because we signed up for a party cruise. Average age is twenty-four. I know that's a bit young for you, but hey, you can still have fun."

Evie closed her eyes and mentally prepared herself for the call from the cruise company to come pick up the Troublesome Trio from whichever port the ship was docked at. Although now that Lexi was married to Noah, he might have better connections and be able to get them home quicker than commercial flights. *Something to bring up to them when they got back.*

A knock sounded at the door. "Hold that thought." Evie went to answer the door, absently pushing back the hair that had escaped her ponytail. They'd rented out the cottage on the back of her grandmother's property and the tenant was due to show up sometime either today or tomorrow. They had no idea who was renting it since a corporation had completed the transaction.

She could see the shadow of a tall man through the frosted glass. Evie had hoped the renter would be a family to distract her grandmother so she might get some rest and not some man to chase around. She opened the door and looked up into the face that haunted Lexi's nightmares. She stifled a scream and started to slam the door on him.

He slapped one strong hand on the door and stopped it from closing. "I'm not him." His low voice with a hint of British accent washed over her. She hesitated for a moment and that was all it took for him to work his way into the house.

"Wait. Don't come any closer. How do I know you aren't him?" She needed to keep him talking to find out if it was Jeremy or Anthony. Her grandmother was just in the other room, hopefully paying attention to what was going on. If it was Jeremy, she could call the police without him knowing. She wasn't sure why Jeremy would come here though, it was Lexi he wanted. If it was Anthony, why was he here?

She watched as he rolled the sleeves up on his arms. She let out a deep breath; there was no scar. She knew what Lexi had done to Jeremy with the cuticle scissors. Since Jeremy hadn't been heard from, and they had been checking hospitals and doctor's offices she knew there was no way a plastic surgeon could have repaired the damage so that nothing was there. She nodded her head trying to still her beating heart. "I suggest you wear short sleeves while you are here, otherwise you're going to have a lot of explaining to do."

"I knew this wasn't going to be easy. You knew that when you sent me that e-mail. If you don't mind, I'd like the keys to the cottage so I can get settled. It's been a long day." He ran his hand through his black, wavy hair.

"Of course, they're just in the living room." Evie turned and walked to the curio cabinet. Thoughts whirled through her mind as she tried to calm her shaking hands. She shivered as he came up behind her.

"You don't have to be scared of me. I'm not here to hurt anyone."

She turned towards him. "That's good, because Lexi has been hurt enough. I know it was no picnic what you went through, but I won't have you hurting her." She stood up to him, secretly liking the fact he was taller than her own six-foot height. Staring into his shocking blue eyes, she couldn't deny how gorgeous he was. He carried himself like he was used to getting what he wanted. "You never replied to my e-mail. So I have no idea why you're here."

"Don't think I haven't done my research before arriving. I know who you are and what Lexi means to you." He took a step closer to her. "But don't think I'm going to let that get in the way of getting the answers I want."

She took a step closer to him so that they were standing toe to toe. "Listen, buster, I'll get in the way if I need to. I'll be keeping an eye on you." She turned back around to get the keys. The next thing she heard was a thunk and a moan. She quickly turned and tried to catch Anthony as he crumpled to the ground.

She landed on her back partially underneath him just catching his head before it hit the ground. Letting out a grunt as his weight pinned her down she looked up at her grandmother who still had the frying pan clutched in her one good hand. "Really?"

Evelyne didn't move. "*Really*? Well, what the hell do you expect me to do when I see this monster standing in my living room hulking over my granddaughter?"

"Didn't you pause to listen what we were talking about before you came out swinging? It's not Jeremy, its Anthony looking for answers, and now he's knocked out on top of me and squashing me."

She lowered the frying pan. "Oh, well, I guess that's not good."

"You think? I could use a little help here." Evie tried not to notice his hard body. Their faces were close to each other. She watched as his eyes started to flutter open. She held her breath wondering what he was going to be like when he woke up.

His words were slurred as he said, "You've got beautiful blue cat eyes. Here kitty-kitty, don't scratch me." His hand came out to brush her hair back. "I can make you purr."

She watched as his eyes rolled back and he passed back out. *Oh shitcrickets, I might be in trouble with this one. Why does he have to be so fucking hot?* She looked up at her grandmother who had a shocked expression on her face and her hand covering her mouth.

"Oh honey, did he just say what I thought he said? We're going to have to watch him. Come on; let's get you up from under him. That is no place for a lady to be."

"Since when did you ever care about acting like a lady?"

"I care about acting like a lady; it's just more fun to say and do what's on my mind at my age." She tilted her head to the side. "You know, he does have a nice ass."

"Not helping." Evie started to wiggle out from under him. It took more effort than she would have thought. She tried not to show how good it felt having his rock hard body on top of hers as she slid out from under his. She needed distance and went into the kitchen to get some cold water thinking she just might need a cold shower. She came back out and dumped it over his head.

Anthony leapt off the floor looking around trying to remember where he was and what dangers could be around. His eyes settled on Evie.

"Anthony, it's ok."

He shook his head to clear it and brought his hands up, his head was throbbing. Once he knew where he was, his heart slowed down. He squinted his eyes at the old lady trying to hide the frying pan behind her back. "I don't think you'll be needing that. I'd appreciate it if you would put it away." He turned to look at Evie. "And if I could have the keys to the cottage please. I'd like to lie down after I make sure the doors are locked." He eyed Evelyne and the frying pan who had the grace to look ashamed.

Evie walked toward him and took his arm. "If you don't mind, I'd like to take a look at your head and get you some aspirin before you leave. It might not be good for you to go to sleep right away."

She led him to the kitchen. He thought it might be better if he could keep an eye on the old lady. "As long as you're sure she's not going to try to poison me, we should be fine." He sat down in the chair and wondered what he had gotten himself into.

He saw Evie give her grandmother a look as she went to the cabinet and got a pill bottle and a glass. He looked at her, not quite trusting, as she filled the glass with water. She took two of the pills and drank them down then handed him the glass and shook out two additional pills. He took them without a word.

Watching as she crossed back over to put the glass in the sink he was startled when the back door burst open and two more old ladies burst in each of them holding a weapon. He quickly jumped up and went around to the other side of the room keeping the table between them all the while his head throbbed in protest of moving so quickly.

"Stop," Evie yelled at them. "It's not what you think."

One of them waved her brass candlestick in the air inching her way into the room. "Let me at the yellow-livered-no-good-scum-sucking-scalawag! I'll show him not to mess with women."

Evie rushed over to stop in front of them. "No, you don't understand, that's not Jeremy."

"You can't be sure. Let us at him, we'll beat the truth out of him." The other one looked dangerous as she swung a baseball bat around.

"Stop it. Listen to me. He's not Jeremy." She turned to Anthony. "Can you please show them your arm? You all know what Lexi did to Jeremy's arm. Anthony doesn't have that scar. There's no way there wouldn't be any damage to his arm at this point. It would be a long, jagged scar, not to mention, we know she went deep enough to ruin the muscle. Chill out." She didn't move until they both lowered their weapons. "Now do you want to explain why you are here acting like a couple of Charlie's Angels?" She crossed her arms across her chest.

Anthony was doing his best to keep up with everything that was happening, but he was a little lost. He tried to remember what he'd learned about Lexi and her friends; he thought these two were Evelyne's friends. Taking a closer look he decided the one with candlestick must be Leigh while the other had to be Marie based on the descriptions he had of them. He just wanted to get out of here with his head still on his shoulders.

Evelyne cleared her throat. "Well, see honey, it's like this. When I got a look at who was at the door, I called the girls to come over for backup."

Evie shook her head. "Shouldn't you have called, oh I don't know, the police? You know, someone *trained*."

The ladies had the decency to look ashamed. Marie sheepishly spoke up. "They don't take our phone calls anymore."

"What? How can that be? No, don't answer, I know why, but they can't do that. This is a perfect example as to why they can't ignore your calls." Evie looked at Anthony. "Sorry, nothing personal, but what if you *had* been Jeremy."

She threw her arms out while talking to the ladies. "So basically you are telling me that you guys could be hurt or in danger and they are just going to leave you hanging? All because you have made a few false reports to get a look at the new young hot recruits? Seriously? I'm going to have a talk with them." She started looking around the kitchen for something, stopping only when Anthony cleared his throat.

"Before you go, can I get the key so that I can get away from Mrs. White, Mrs. Peacock and Miss Scarlett before they decide to play a live version of Clue? Mrs. White already tried to kill me in the living room with a frying pan."

Leigh pumped her fist in the air. "Woo-hoo, I'm Miss Scarlett."

Evelyne shook her head. "Why do you get to be Miss Scarlett? I want to be Miss Scarlett. Mrs. White is boring." She looked at Leigh and they smiled. "I know. Marie can be Mrs. White. She'd like that better than being known as Mrs. Peacock. And we know I love the cock."

Anthony shook his head not believing what he just heard. He felt like he was being tossed around in a storm. He watched Evie laughing and something stirred in his chest. She was drop-dead gorgeous, tall, and loyal. He was amazed at how quickly she jumped to the defense of people. Even him, after only knowing he was Anthony, and not Jeremy, for a short time. He watched the sway of her hips as she walked out of the room. When she came back a few minutes later, she never broke eye contact. He liked the fact that she didn't seem to back down easy. He was getting lost in her, and the magic she wove with those cat eyes. He had to get out of this house.

"Here you go." She dropped the keys in his hand and handed him some papers. "I printed out information on concussions. Make sure you follow what they tell you to do. If you have any symptoms that they list, come get me, and I'll take you to the hospital. Lexi and Noah are still on their honeymoon. I'd appreciate it if you let me talk to her first before you go barging in there."

"What makes you think I'd go barging in there?" When she didn't say anything, just staring at him with a look of disbelief on her face, he continued. "Fine, I thought they were due back yesterday."

"Do I want to know how you found out about that? It's not exactly public knowledge." She shook her head. "Never mind. They decided to stay a week or two longer. I'll have a talk with Lexi when she gets back. This is something that has to be done in person and not over the phone. I'm not going to ruin her honeymoon because of Jeremy. He's taken enough from her already. Now let me show you to the cottage so you can get settled and we can talk more, later."

Very quickly she showed him to the cottage not saying much. Once he was inside she left quickly. The next thing Anthony knew he was left alone looking at the back of the closed door. He walked to the window and watched her walking back towards the main house. He wasn't sure where this journey was going to take him but by the looks of it, it was going to be one hell of a ride.

– CHAPTER TWO –

Anthony's head was feeling better but there was still a dull ache behind his eyes. He couldn't believe that old lady knocked him over the head. He had hoped this would be a quick trip, find out what Evie was up to and talk to Lexi, then out. He knew that it wasn't her fault he went to prison, but it still angered him that he wasn't able to prove his innocence, that most people believed he was capable of something like that. He learned quickly who his friends were and who just wanted something out of him.

He'd spread out the papers on top of the small table off the kitchen in the cottage. He looked around wondering where else he could put them. He might have to go get some tacks and put things up on the walls. He wasn't worried about any damage; he would pay to have them repaired.

He had spent hours going over everything his people could dig up on Jeremy Ellison. It wasn't pretty. It seems that Jeremy was responsible for

Tiffani's murder all those years ago. He felt an ache in his heart thinking about her. He wouldn't say he loved her, but he cared for her. But love? No.

As far as Anthony could tell, Jeremy had been following him for years, and possibly killing women that got too close or fit a certain description. His men were still going back through everything to see if there were any strange disappearances or murders in and around the time that Anthony was traveling.

He started pacing the room. *How could I have been so stupid not to realize someone was following me and murdering women?* He shook his head; he couldn't dwell on that. He had to look forward to finding this bastard and giving him what he deserves.

His thoughts were interrupted by a knock. Scowling he went to the door and opened it. There stood Evie, the setting sun shining through the clouds behind her. He was taken aback by her beauty and more harshly than intended said, "What?" He watched as she took a step back.

"Dinner's ready," she said. When he didn't say anything she continued, "It states in the rental agreement that dinner is included. So," she gestured with her hand towards the house, "dinner is ready."

He nodded. "If you don't mind, I think I'll skip it." He started to close the door.

Evie stepped forward essentially blocking him from shutting the door. "You might want to reconsider. If you don't, they're just going to find another way to grill you. I'm sure The Trio is in your reports, and I can guarantee there is no way it could cover everything they've done. They will let nothing stop them until they get answers. Get it out of the way now and they might leave you alone. You really don't know what they're capable of."

Anthony stood there and tried to remember what his research had said about the old ladies. He was beginning to think he should have paid more attention to that part. He sighed. "Fine, just let me lock up."

"You don't have to do that. We don't have a lot of crime around here."

"If it's all the same to you, I will. Jeremy is out there somewhere and I don't want him in there."

"You're right."

Walking toward the house, he was happy she didn't try to fill the silence with nonsense. He just wanted to get this over with and back to figuring out what Jeremy's next step might be.

He wondered when she would bring up the e-mail she sent to him. It had kept him up many a night as he tried to figure out what to do. Now that he was here he just wanted to get started. He felt frustrated that Lexi wasn't here.

He walked into the room and took a mouth-watering deep breath of what was sure to be pot roast. He readied himself for the lion's den. The three of them stood together on the other side of the table, their hands folded in front of them, attempting to look demure.

"I take it the weapons are locked up?"

Leigh moved forward and held out her hand to him. "Hey toots, I'm Leigh, sorry I didn't introduce myself earlier. Yes, Evie took them away from us. Some nonsense about hurting ourselves."

Solemnly shaking her hand he said, "I'm Anthony. I'm glad you no longer look like you want to bash my head in."

Marie came up to him and looked at him through squinted eyes. "You've got some good bones and nice muscles. We'll see what the personality's like. I'm Marie."

He didn't know what to think of these women. Looking over to Evie he saw her trying to hide a smile behind her hand and narrowed his eyes at her. Suddenly his face was gripped by strong fingers and he was forced to look into the eyes of one pissed off grandmother.

Speaking in a soft tone so that only he could hear her Evelyne forced him to bend down so that they were eye to eye. "Listen buster, you'd better be nice to that little girl over there otherwise smacking you upside your head with a frying pan will be the least of your worries." Giving his face a little shake, she let him go.

"Okay, let's eat." Evie said in an overly cheerful voice.

He walked over to the only chair that's back faced the wall and sat down so the ladies couldn't sneak up behind him. "Do I have to worry about the food being poisoned?"

Leigh gasped. "Don't ever say such a thing! Wasting perfectly good food? Never." She piled heap upon heap of food on her plate.

He still held back and waited until they all started eating before he began. He closed his eyes when he tasted the food. Being locked up for five years he missed real food, especially home cooked. It was something he wasn't going to take for granted any longer. Among other things…

He looked up when one of the women cleared their throat. Looking at each of them, he couldn't guess the problem. "What?"

"Well, why don't you tell us about yourself?" asked Marie.

"What do you want to know that you haven't already read in the papers?"

With a sly look towards Evie, Leigh said, "Well, we really don't know much about you. Just the things that have to do with that nasty Jeremy, and of course, Lexi. But what about you, where did you grow up, what are your plans, you know, things about you."

Anthony sighed. He really didn't want to talk about his life with these women. Looking at their hopeful faces, he knew they just wanted to try and figure things out and why he was here. He looked at Evie and thought she just might be right; it *would* be easier to just tell them what they wanted to know and get it over with

Starting with the easy things, he went back to the past. "I was born in Washington D.C., but my parents spent a lot of time between the States and London. My family has been in the import/export business for generations. When my father took over he wanted to expand, hence spending time here."

"So then you traveled a lot when you were younger?" asked Leigh. "I always loved to travel."

"Yes, we were a family, just the three of us, and they wanted to make sure that we stayed together as much as possible. When I got older, I wanted to spread my wings so I spent some time in the Seattle area on my own." He became quiet and reflective.

Softly Evie asked, "Is that where you met Tiffani?"

He looked deep into her eyes. "Yes. It wasn't love. I was just enjoying myself, as she was also. We both knew what the score was. What we didn't know was how seriously messed up her ex was."

"Have you been able to find out anything about him?"

"Some. After Tiffani was killed I went back to London to stay with my parents for a while. I needed something stable. Sadly, I had some losses soon after that."

He paused and looked down where Evie had reached over and grabbed his hand. His heart contracted at the simple, compassionate gesture on her part. Pushing away the thoughts as to why it meant so much to him he continued. "So I traveled more. Never staying in one place too long. I was lucky and Neil, the man who was running the family company was competent, so I left everything up to him."

"Does he still run it?" asked Evelyne.

"As of right now he does. After traveling, I decided it was time I step up and take over the company. He retired and I had a good run, until the trial." He paused, not sure how much to say. "Well, he came back and has been running things until I get this all cleared up."

Leigh clapped her hands together. "All right, this is what I have been waiting for. What is your plan? What can we do to help? When do we start?"

Anthony glanced over at Evie who was trying not to laugh. "*My* plan is to meet with Lexi." Hearing Evie's gasp he quickly continued, "Of course, I would want to talk to Noah first, let him know what I want to do and help prepare Lexi for seeing me."

"Excuse me? Talk to Noah first? Why? Because she's a weak little woman and wouldn't be able to make a decision on her own?"

"No, you can get down off of your chair and stop pumping your fist at the injustice towards women. I want to talk to Noah first because I feel that it would be better coming from him than me just showing up at their door one day."

Watching as she crossed her arms across her chest, he appreciated how her breasts pushed up and stretched her shirt tight against them.

"The reason I want to talk to Lexi is to see if there is anything else that I might be able to say to her that might trigger something that she forgot from her two meetings with Jeremy. She is the only link that I have to him. I have to find him. He has to be stopped."

"Well, you're certainly right there. Now what can we do to help? You know we want that bastard caught just as much as you." Evelyne had a truly scary look on her face and Anthony was happy he wasn't on receiving end of it.

"*You* ladies aren't part of the plan. I can do this all on my own." Looking at their faces he thought it would be best if he added, "But thank you. If I need anything, you'll be the first people I call."

"You'd better call. Just because we're old doesn't mean we can't kick some ass." Leigh got up and proceeded to showcase her high kicks. Unfortunately, she was looking at Anthony more than where she was kicking and ended up kicking the bakers rack. "Oops. Well, in a fight I'd be more focused."

"You know Anthony, we've all taken self-defense classes. After what happened to Lexi we felt it was something we needed to know. We don't get as much practice as we'd like, but Evie here, well, she's really good. In fact, she goes every week and is so good, she helps teach other women." Marie said.

"That's very wise, ladies. You always need to be prepared."

"Well, we would go more, but for some reason they like to have women teach the classes. If there are guys, they're under all that padding. So now we just go whenever they're having a guest instructor that just happens to be a hot guy." Evelyne licked her lips.

"Oh Evelyne, remember the last one. Oh my. I didn't think I'd be able to make it through the class without combusting. He was so cut, and when he took his shirt off, his vee, oh my, I thought I was going to have an orgasm just looking at him." Leigh fanned herself.

Anthony was taking a drink and almost spit his water out across the table. Instead, he ended up swallowing wrong and coughing.

Evie started thumping him on the back, he looked at her out the corner of his eye when she started laughing. Catching his look, she just shrugged.

Evelyne stood up and walked over to the counter. "Speaking of orgasms, who is ready for dessert? My world famous strawberry shortcake, guaranteed to please you."

"Umm… thanks, I think. But I really should be going."

"Oh come on honey, live a little. We'll give you some extra cream."

"Seriously, I really need to go." He stood up and walked quickly to the door. Turning towards them he said, "Thank you for an interesting meal."

He didn't close the door quick enough before hearing one of them say, "Damn. You were right, Evelyne. He does have a nice ass. I'd love to smack that."

~*~

After dinner, Evie was enjoying a glass of wine while swinging gently in the hammock looking up at the stars. Thinking about the ramifications of Anthony showing up and what that would mean to Lexi and why he hadn't said anything about her e-mail. *There has to be something I can do to help.* She would do anything for her family and friends even if it meant working with someone whose face haunted Lexi's nightmares. It was going to take some work, but she would have to keep Anthony and Jeremy separated. Because she would do anything to help her friend and if she projected Jeremy's evilness onto Anthony that wouldn't be good. He was his own man.

Could she really do it? Would he allow her to help? What would it be like to work closely with him? All the different scenarios went through her mind trying to think of every possible angle before forcing him to let her help. It was a shame he was so hot, it sure was going to make things interesting.

Chuckling to herself at what the Troublesome Trio said to Anthony over dinner, she didn't hear his approach.

"Hello, Evie," he said while he leaned up against the tree at her feet.

She jumped and almost spilled her wine. "Jesus, wear a fucking bell next time." She tried to be sly about checking out his arm but when he simply moved his arm so she could get a better look she knew she'd have to get better about checking out if it was him or Jeremy.

"Sorry." She shrugged. "I have to know it's you and not him."

He shoved off of the tree and started pacing. "Do you know what it is like for me? Every time I look in the mirror I know that women looked at this face before they were killed by that bastard. I have people looking at me all the time wondering who it is standing there in front of them. He took people I cared for from me. He took five years of my life from me."

She couldn't imagine what it must be like for him; especially knowing Jeremy was out there somewhere waiting to strike. She wanted to comfort him, but had no idea how. "What are you going to do?"

He spun towards her stalking until he was inches from her. "What do you think I'm going to do? Anything and everything I can to end his life. Make him pay for everything he's taken from me."

She folded her arms across her chest. "And what? Damn everyone who gets in your way?"

"Precisely."

"What if you had someone to help you?"

"I don't need help."

"Yes, you do. You're too close to this."

"And you're not?"

"Only in the fact this happened to my best friend. I didn't lose everything you did. I wasn't attacked two times. I might see something you would miss. You both deserve the peace that comes with knowing this piece of shit is locked up."

"No." He turned and started to walk away.

Standing there with her mouth open at the audacity of him she dropped her wine glass in the grass and ended up having to run to catch up with him. She moved to block his way placing a hand on his chest. "Listen, buster, either you let me help you or I will do it on my own, and not share my information with you. You had your chance when I e-mailed you a month ago. I've heard nothing since then."

"What information could you have that I don't already have?"

"Keep acting like a stubborn mule and you'll never know what I've got. You forget, I have access to all of Noah's information, and his team has dug up a lot." She stood there holding her ground hoping he wouldn't call her bluff. As of right now, she hadn't exactly seen anything from Noah's men, but she was hoping he'd let her see everything, especially if Anthony agreed to let her help.

"Why did you come up and talk to me just now? You could have just turned around and I would have never known. You're seeking me out for some reason. What is it you want?" Evie demanded.

He picked her up and moved her out of the way. She stood there watching him stride towards the cottage never looking back.

Bastard. I'll show him. She stalked back and picked up the wine glass. *Shit. That was my favorite Callaway Sauvignon Blanc wine, too.* Picking up the phone in her room, she started making calls.

– CHAPTER THREE –

Anthony spent most of night going over everything he'd found regarding Jeremy Ellison. He hated to admit to himself, but maybe there was other information out there that he hadn't been able to find.

Maybe Evie would have something that would help. He opened up the e-mail she'd sent him. She had reached out to him hoping that they could work together to find Jeremy. He'd decided to show up on her doorstep to keep her off balance and maybe have the upper hand.

Not wanting to dwell on the fact that he was charmed by Evie, he shifted gears and thought about how this whole investigation might affect her. Even though she didn't fit the profile that Jeremy liked to kill, that doesn't mean that he wouldn't go after her if he thought she was too close to Anthony.

Knowing that she would go off on her own he decided it would be better if they did team up. At least that way, he'd be able to keep an eye on her.

He found her sitting on a lonely stretch of beach not too far from her grandmother's house staring at the waves crashing on the sand the next morning. He came up and sat down beside her. She didn't turn to look at him. This was going to be more difficult than he first thought. Clearing his throat to get her attention, he began. "Can I start by saying that I'm sorry for how I acted last night?"

She turned to look at him briefly before looking back at the ocean.

"Okay, I was completely out of line. You're just trying to help and I threw it back in your face." He waited for her to say something, when she didn't, he knew he was in trouble and it pissed him off. "You can sit there and sulk like a child or we can start going over what we each have, to find out where he might be hiding or what he's going to do next."

"*Sulking like a child?* Is this how you apologize and ask for my help? You need to work on your approach because it seriously sucks ass." She stood up and started to walk away from him.

"Shit." He stood and stalked towards her grabbing her arm and swung her back around to face him. "Do I need to point out that running away is also acting like a child?"

He could see her face flush with anger and her eyes become lasers boring into him. He could feel the heat coming off of her in waves.

"Do *I* need to point out that you did the exact same thing last night?"

"Touché. Now that we've got that out of the way, can we talk about what we should do next?" It had been so long since he'd been with a woman and this one was making him crazy even in the short amount of time they had known each other.

"We both want the same thing, so why are you making this so difficult? I would think you'd want as much help as possible."

"I do. I spent a lot of time thinking last night and you are right."

She held up a hand. "Wait, can you repeat that?" She grinned at him.

He playfully knocked her shoulder back, "No. Anyway, it would be stupid not to pool our resources and see if we can figure things out." He held his hand out to her. "So, partners?"

Grinning she ignored his hand and jumped into his arms. He took a step back trying to keep them both from tumbling back into the sand. The little he knew about her was that she was impulsive, but even her jumping into his arms shocked him. Add the fact that she felt so good in his arms he was more than just physically off-balance.

"Let's do this!" She jumped down out of his arms and pulled on his hand dragging him back to the cottage. "Come on, let's get started. We are so going to catch this bastard. I can feel it."

He couldn't believe how good she felt in his arms, however brief it was, and it left him wanting more. In the past, he'd always dated women that he knew where they were coming from. With Evie, it could change from one second to the next. He had no idea where this journey was going to take them but he was willing to bet it would be one hell of a ride.

Evie dashed into her grandmother's house to make sure she was fine and didn't need anything before she ran up to her room to grab the information on both Anthony and Jeremy which Noah's man, Bruno, had sent over last night. Lucky for her, she'd charmed Bruno when Lexi was recovering; he sent her everything without questioning it. He'd just made her promise she wasn't going to do anything stupid. Since she didn't plan on it, she should be keeping that promise.

On her way back out to Anthony's, she grabbed a large thermos and filled it with coffee. Having spent most of the night awake going over all the paperwork, she was tired. She was going to need to be on the top of her game if Anthony was going to allow her to continue to help.

"Do you need a condom?"

Evie stopped in her tracks and spun around to face her grandmother. "What are you talking about?"

"Do you think I've gotten to this age and not know what happens between an attractive man and woman when they start to spend a lot of time together?

"Especially when one of them goes running out after the other one spent all morning looking for her and the other one comes back grinning like the Cheshire cat?" Evelyne crossed her arms over her chest.

"Grams, it's not like that. We are going to work together to find Jeremy. The last thing I need is a man in my life right now."

"That's exactly when it happens. Now as much as I want to be a great-grandmother, I would appreciate it if you did it in the correct order."

Rolling her eyes towards the ceiling she hoped for strength. "I'll take that under advisement. Now, we've got a lot of papers to go through." She started walking towards the door.

"So you don't find him attractive at all?"

Sighing she turned back around to face her grandmother. "Yes, of course, I'd have to be dead to not think he was attractive. I've learned my appreciation for men from you. But that's all it will be. Happy?"

"No, not at all, but you'll do what you want. You've always done that. But here." Evelyne tossed a strip of condoms to Evie. "You'll want these."

Catching them easily she shook her head and turned around and shoved them in the closest drawer.

"Later, Grams." She ran out the door before her grandmother could force them back on her.

~*~

They spent the first couple of hours reading the information the other had. Evie sighed and threw the papers down next to her on the couch.

Anthony looked up at her. He got up and went to the fridge where he pulled out a bottle of white wine and poured her a glass.

"How did you know I needed a drink?" She closed her eyes and enjoyed the first crisp taste of it.

"Just a lucky guess. Find anything interesting?"

"Not really. It seems like we have about the same information. I was hoping something would jump out at me, but so far nothing."

"Same here. As far as we can tell, and from what Jeremy said, Tiffani was the first." He walked over to a map he'd just hung on the wall. There were pins in about a half a dozen cities and pointed to Seattle. "He said that there were others between her and Lexi. There were some reports of women matching the description gone missing or being found dead around the same I time I was there."

Evie got up from the couch and stood beside him tapping England. "Here, this was next. This was an ex-girlfriend of yours right?"

"Yes. Natalie. Natalie Sutton. We dated in school. Really nothing serious. We'd known each other for a long time; we ended up more like best friends than anything else. After Tiffani, she was there for me. We'd just spend time together. It was good, familiar, a friend that was there for me."

She laid her head on his shoulder, feeling the pain he'd gone through, admiring his strength at fighting to find the answers no matter what.

"Her parents had a country house; we spent a lot of time out there. We'd sit under this one tree and talk for hours or read. She was like family to me. They found her up in that tree. Well, parts of her. He cut her up into pieces and placed them on different branches. I will never forget the sight or what the bark on the tree looked like with the blood seeping into it."

Shivering at the thought of it, she rubbed his back. "I'm so sorry, Anthony." She could feel him turn his head to look down at her.

"It's not your fault."

Lifting her head off of his shoulder, she looked at him. "I know, but still, no one should go through that."

She could feel a change in the air, as if everything pulled away and it was just the two of them. No other sounds came through but their breathing.

She was drowning in the beauty of his shocking, bright, blue eyes. It was such a contrast to his tanned skin and dark hair. Slowly, she reached up and laid her hand gently on the side of his face. His arm slid around her waist and pulled her closer to him. She breathed in the scent of his cologne, intoxicating her.

He dipped his head, bringing his lips closer, never taking his eyes off of hers. His other hand came up, slid around to the back of her neck and his fingers wove into her hair.

She reached up, running her hand over his arm, feeling his muscles move and play responding to her touch. Without hesitation, she moved towards him closing the gap between their lips. Just as they touched the sound of a door banging close by made them jump apart.

They stood staring at each other, their chests rising and falling, trying to catch their breaths. Evie couldn't believe she almost kissed him. Serious, curl your toes kind of kiss. Her body felt heavy with want. Needing distance, she stepped away and went over to the table where there were photos laid out. "Ok, well, where were we?"

It was something she didn't want to look at, but felt that she had to. They were crime scene photos. She picked up a photo that showed a tree. Setting it aside, she picked up the next one. This one showed a woman that had been twisted and broken in ways that weren't natural. She was skewered through metal sculpture at an art gallery.

Anthony walked over to see what see was looking at. "That was Monique Diaz. She was a model and full of life. I was only in Paris for a short period of time; we went to that art opening together. They found her like that a couple of days later. There was an emergency at the London house so I'd left earlier than originally scheduled. I was never questioned since it was documented I was already out of the country. This was one of the ones that I didn't know about until after Jeremy told Lexi there had been others."

"Who was next?" Evie didn't want to look at any more pictures, but she knew she had to. She also knew that she was going to be having nightmares tonight.

"Chelle Michaels. She was in L.A. for a teacher's conference, originally from Pittsburg. We were staying at the same hotel. There was a mix-up and they ended up booking us in the same suite. She was very understanding about it, she was supposed to be in a regular room, the hotel didn't have any available. Since it was a two bedroom suite, we ended up sharing it for a night. I checked out early and let her have it. They found her two days later in the room. It seems that her whole family is in law enforcement, they made sure that all of the photos and reports were sealed. I don't have much on her. At the time of death, I was in a meeting surrounded by other people, so nothing came of it."

Evie was thankful for one less crime scene she had to look at. Hearing about the lives they lived before being brutally murdered made the weight of what they were trying to accomplish even heavier.

Placing another smiling photo in front of her, Anthony continued. "Then we have Heather Roberts. A kick-boxing instructor from Phoenix, Arizona. She was on vacation in the Caribbean. We met at a club one night, hit it off. We were supposed to meet the next day and go sailing. She never showed up. I just figured I'd been stood up. This was another one I didn't know anything about. It seems she's still missing. Since she fits the profile, we can only assume that Jeremy was there, too."

"Oh no! Her poor family. What they must be going through." Evie didn't want to think about it.

"It seems that he took a break while I was in prison. So the next one is Christina Cooper, the one found at the carnival. She liked men and was a little wild."

"Maybe we could go talk to her ex-husband? Since we have extra time before Lexi and Noah get home, we shouldn't waste it."

"What could he tell us?"

"Who knows, but it's better than just sitting around reading these reports over and over. Maybe we can get some little piece of information. Every little piece helps the puzzle come together. We should also go to motels around the area and talk to people who rented him rooms. We've gone over all of the police investigations, including the international ones. Maybe we can find something they couldn't. I know, it's a long shot, but we don't have to worry about protocol."

He sighed. "Well, you are right in the fact that it would be better than just sitting around waiting. So we start tomorrow?"

"Sounds good. Now, I'm sorry, but I need a break and it's getting late. I think we should call it a night."

He followed her to the door. "Evie, thank you." When she started to shake her head, he stopped her. "Don't say it's nothing, because you know it isn't. I really appreciate what you are doing not just for Lexi, but for me, too. She's got a very special friend in you."

"I'd do this for anyone."

"Yes, I believe you would. Now try to get some sleep and forget about this for a little bit."

She turned and walked out the door. With the screen door between them, she placed her hand on the screen. "Good night."

Placing his hand on hers he said, "Good night, la mia belezza."

Evie walked away feeling his eyes on her, repeating the words he said to her all the way up to her room. As soon as she closed the door, she went to her computer and searched for the meaning of his words. She sighed at the translation, *my beauty.*

Jeremy sat back in the dirty motel room staring at the computer screen. Things couldn't be going better. Anthony had come to Ipswich. As far as he could tell, he didn't have any security with him. *Now to have some fun.*

– CHAPTER FOUR –

"**O**K, we're here, what's the big emergency?" Leigh said as she and Marie walked into the kitchen at Evelyne's house.

"I have no idea what little Miss Thing is up to," said Evelyne as she handed them both a cup of coffee.

Evie breezed into the room and got a soda out of the fridge. "Good, you're all here. Let's get down to it."

"I'd like to get down to it, but this is slowing me down." Evelyne wiggled her arm.

Evie gave her a look. "Haven't you learned anything after the last time?"

"Nope."

"Anyway, I need your help. As you know, Anthony is here to find out as much as he can about Jeremy. We spent last night going over all of each other's information. We decided to work together to try to find him."

Evelyne jumped up and started pacing the room. "Are you kidding me? Have you thought this thing through? No, of course not. You always leap before you think."

"I wonder where she gets it from," whispered Leigh to Marie.

"I heard that! Do you have any idea what could happen to you? And what about Lexi? How is she going to feel about this?"

"Grandma, calm down. Yes, I have thought this through. I know the risks, but really what else could I do? He's an innocent man that has had a lot of bad things happen to him, and someone is out there planning on causing more pain. It's not just about Lexi anymore. They *both* deserve that bastard be locked up where he can't hurt anyone anymore. You all know I've always loved puzzles, I think this is something that I could help with. Please try to understand."

"Honey, we are, but you've got to give us more." Leigh rubbed Evie's back.

Evie stood up and walked over to where her grandmother was leaning against the counter and grabbed her hands. "You *know* me. You know that I can take care of myself. You know that I have always been the one to figure out who did it before anyone else when watching a movie or reading a book. I might be able to see something that other people can't. While yes, I do tend to leap before I look, that isn't always a bad thing. Besides, Anthony and I will be together. I'll try to make sure I'm not alone. Please understand."

"I think it's a good idea," Marie said.

"What? How can you say that?" Evelyne demanded.

"Think about what she said. Take the emotion of the fact she is your granddaughter out of it. Another pair of eyes won't hurt anything. Besides, we might learn more, Anthony might have some information Noah's man wasn't able to dig up. The more we know, the better. They can do things that law enforcement can't. Lexi will be home soon. It would be nice if we could take this one thing off of her so she wouldn't have to stress about Jeremy still being out there. And like Evie said, Anthony doesn't deserve this. What has happened to him is wrong; she can help make it right."

Evelyne's eyes were narrowed and her jaw was set. "What about Lexi? Have you thought about that?"

"Oh course, I have. I know seeing Anthony is going to be a huge shock. I'm hoping that telling her before seeing him will help. She's got Noah; you know he'd do anything for her. She knows that there is a difference between the two. She wants this as much for her as for Anthony. She still feels terrible about her part in the whole thing. She's strong enough to get through this, I know it."

"And there is nothing going on between the two of you?" Marie asked.

Evie tried to make sure her face didn't show anything. In fact, that kept her up more than the nightmares of what she'd seen and they'd talked about. "Of course not."

38

"Evie, honey, we aren't stupid." Leigh said.

"What are you guys talking about?"

Leigh started ticking off on her fingers, "First, the two of you kept looking at each other all through dinner the other night." Before Evie could interrupt she continued, "Second, he went searching for you all over the place the next day, then you two spend hours together alone. Finally, you are doing whatever you can to help him, even putting yourself in danger. That adds up to something going on. Besides, even though the killer has his face, you have to admit, he's pretty hot. There is something about how he carries himself. You can tell he's used to being in charge, giving orders and getting what he wants. There is something animalistic about it. You just know he'd be great in the sack."

Evie tried to keep her imagination in check as the others laughed and agreed.

"You guys don't have to worry about me. I've got this." Evie only hoped it was true. She was afraid of what might happen between them and what it could mean to the people she loved.

When they pulled into a motel parking lot, Evie turned to Anthony. "Now, let me do this. You stay here, I've got a plan."

Grabbing her arm before she could make a move to scoot out of the car, he had her look at him. "What do you mean 'you've got a plan' Why didn't you share this with me?"

"Because I knew you'd try to stop me."

"I can still stop you."

"But you won't." She batted her eyelashes at him and laughed when he growled at her. "Seriously, look here." She handed him her phone and tapped an app on. Up on the screen came a view out the front windshield of the car.

"What in the hell?" He looked at her when he heard his voice come out of the phone.

"See I've got this hooked up so you will be able to see and hear everything that I'm doing." When he didn't say anything she just looked at him and said, "Well, where are the protests now?"

"Give me a minute. I'll think of something."

"Nope, I've got to get going. I've done my research, Hank is in there now. He's a middle-aged good-ole boy who likes the ladies." She unbuttoned a couple of buttons on her shirt so that her cleavage was showing. When he growled again she looked at him while fluffing her hair up. "What? I'll have him eating out of my hand in no time."

"That's what I am afraid of. How did you know this person would be there?" He watched in fascination as she applied a bright red lipstick to her lips.

She leaned over close to him and patted his cheek. "You're not the only one who can do research. Be a good boy and stay here." She threw back her head and laughed as he growled again. "Now, watch me work."

She got out of the car and with an extra sway to her hips, she walked towards the motel office.

Evie took a deep breath before entering the office. Squaring her shoulders so her boobs stood out even more than usual and she added a small flirty smile as she opened the door. She was satisfied that it was working by the way Hank's eyes bulged almost out of his head.

"Hey darling." She said playing up her Boston accent as she crossed to the counter and leaned over the counter so he would have the perfect shot down her shirt. "I was wondering if you could help me."

"Umm… sure… what can I… umm… do for you?" He rubbed his hand over his lunch stained shirt that was stretched tight over his belly.

Evie looked around before leaning even further over and dropping her voice. "Are we the only ones here? No one else can hear us right?"

Coughing, he tried to recover quickly, "Yes, it's just us. How can I do you? I mean what can I do for you?"

She let a high-pitched giggle come out and covered his arm with her hand and started rubbing it. "Well, see, I'm so embarrassed. This was a mistake."

"No, honey, don't worry about it. I want to help, tell me what you need."

She wanted to shiver and get as far away from his leering as she could, but she knew she had to finish what she started for Lexi. "So I think my loser of a fiancé is cheating on me. The guy is loaded, so if he is, I want proof so I can get my cut, you understand?" When he nodded she continued. "No one treats me that way. I want him to pay, with money. So, I was wondering if you could take a look at this guy and tell me if you've seen him around, and if he ever had a chick with him."

She slid the picture of Anthony across the counter, it was the best they could do since they didn't have anything good of Jeremy. Watching as his shaking fingers picked up the picture, she held her breath hoping for some kind of information they could use.

"Hmmm, yeah, he's been here."

Evie moved and covered her mouth with her hand jabbing her fingernail into the underside of her chin effectively making her eyes tear. "Oh no!"

He took one pudgy hand and awkwardly patted her shoulder. "Honey, it's not that bad. I remember him from last year. He paid cash, stayed for about a week. He didn't bring any woman by."

She opened her eyes wide. "Really? Are you sure? How can you remember?"

He turned red and rubbed his hand over the back of his neck. "Well, see, he's not the typical clientele I get here. You could tell he was used to money. He had to have his room cleaned at a specific time every day and a certain way, otherwise, there was, I don't know, a coldness to him if it wasn't right."

Sighing she said, "That does sound like him."

He leaned over the counter to get closer to her. "You know, you don't need him, you need a real man, one that would treat you like the queen you are."

"Did he leave anything behind?"

"Nope, in fact I think that was the cleanest the room had ever been. Now honey, why don't you come back here and let me take care of you."

Evie knew it was time to make a retreat. "Thanks for the info, hun. I've got to go." She turned and walked quickly out the door ignoring his pleas for her to come back.

"Where to now?" Anthony asked.

"What climbed up your ass?"

"Gee, I don't know. Your little performance?"

"Oh come on, we got the information we needed."

"Yeah, in about another thirty seconds I was going to have to come in there, then what would you have done?"

"I'd have figured something out. Anyway, let's go to this little B&B up the road a bit." She took a brush out of her purse and started to comb her hair.

"What no hoochi-mama this time?"

She burst out laughing. "Hoochi-mama? Oh god. That is hysterical in your slightly proper British accent."

"Can we get back to business?"

"Sure can, Sweet Cheeks." She enjoyed pushing his buttons and wondered how far she could push before he pushed back.

"Here make yourself useful, plug in the address in the GPS."

"Oh, I'm very useful." She put the address into the GPS. "There. It's not too far away. It's lucky we know his real name and that he didn't use something different."

"Hopefully that will be his undoing; he's a bit too cocky for his own good."

She watched as his knuckles became white on the steering wheel. Wanting to sooth him and take his pain away she reached over and placed her hand on his shoulder. "I know Anthony, we'll catch him. He can't keep this up forever."

"But how many other women have to die first? How many more is he going to torture?"

"We just have to work harder. We've got to do this."

They rode the rest of the way in silence.

~*~

Anthony looked over at Evie who looked like her normal self again, wondering what she was going to do this time. "Don't do anything stupid." That last one had almost given him a heart attack.

"Who me? Come on, out of everything, this is the easiest part. Chill dude." She chuckled as she got out of the car and slammed the door shut.

He turned to the app on the phone and watched the B&B come into view. He didn't want her to know how much he worried about her, or how amusing she was. Sitting back, he got comfortable to enjoy the show.

Walking into the foyer Evie looked around and marveled at the detail in the restored, old, Victorian house. Everything stayed true to the historic value, but had been updated to include all of the modern conveniences. She turned when she heard someone approaching. *Show time.*

"Hello dear, how may we help you?" asked the man with dark close-cut hair and green eyes.

She ran her fingers through her hair and then made a helpless gesture with her hands.

Another man who also had close-cut hair, except his was dark blonde. He had brown eyes and a goatee. As he came over, he put his arm around her. "Oh, now, it can't be that bad. Let's just go sit down in the parlor for a bit and we'll get to know each other. Good idea, Joe?"

Evie didn't miss the look that passed between them. *So far so good.*

"I'll get us some tea, and maybe some cookies?"

Seeing Evie nod, he left the room. She let the other man lead her to the sofa and sat down with him.

"Okay girlfriend, you've got a couple of minutes to pull yourself together before Joe gets back so I'll tell you everything you need to know about us while we wait. My name is Amir. Joe and I have owned this place for, oh, about five years now. We took a couple of years to restore it."

"It looks wonderful. You did a great job."

"I can't take credit for the work, I'm the idea man, now my Joe he's the one with the good hands."

"Here we are. Now you sit back and have a snack and tell us what you need." Joe set everything down on the coffee table.

"Thank you. Well, I'm not sure where to begin."

"At the beginning, of course." Amir laughed.

"Well, I understand this is a bed and breakfast that caters to the gay community. Right?"

"Yes dear, we aren't exclusive toward the community, but yes, most of our guests are gay. We like to support tolerance no matter what the lifestyle." Joe patted her hand.

"Well, I think my fiancé is cheating on me. I have felt that something has been off for a while. I checked his receipts, and well, he stayed here for a bit. I was wondering if you could help me. Have you seen this man? He would have stayed here last year." She made sure her hand shook as she gave them the photo.

Joe looked at Amir before turning to her. "Well my dear, you don't have a very nice fiancé."

"Why do you say that?"

Amir picked up his tea. "It's not because he had to have everything a certain way and at specific times. But well, in our situation you have to be in tune to other people. Unfortunately, there are always people who may want to hurt us because they consider us 'different.' We could tell he was disgusted by us and the other people renting rooms here. He wanted nothing to do with us. There was something dark about him. We had to ask him to leave."

"He never brought anyone here?"

"No honey, he didn't. He only ended up staying for two nights, but was booked for a whole week. While the revenue would be nice, he booked our largest room, we don't need his negativity here," Joe said.

"I'm so sorry about that, but thank you, I needed to know that. It seems he's hiding more than I originally thought." She wanted to keep as close to the truth as possible. "One of my employees is gay and since my business is a huge part of my life, so is Jesse. I can't have anyone in my life that isn't accepting. Thank you for your time." She stood up to leave. "You really have a nice place here. I wish you success."

"Thank you, hon, and be sure to come back. We'll even give you a discount." Amir winked at her.

~*~

Anthony and Evie were silent on the drive to the marina. Anthony was trying to process everything he had heard. When they were almost there, Anthony reached over and grabbed her hand. "I'm sorry. I know Jesse means a lot to you, and you hate to see that kind of intolerance."

She looked over at him and he could see the pain in her eyes. "I just don't know how people can be so mean. If everyone would just be a little nicer and more accepting of people, this world would be a better place."

Gently, he squeezed her hand. "Yes, it would. Maybe someday."

"And we really didn't learn anything new."

"Maybe at this next stop. Do you have a plan for this one?" He was hoping to get her mind off of how Jeremy had treated the owners of the B&B.

"Of course, I always have a plan."

From what he could tell, half the time she would follow her heart before her head. "Really?" He said sarcastically.

"Well, most of the time anyway." She shrugged. "The rental place is owned by Susan. It used to be her and her husband's before he died. Now it's just her. I'll be back in a bit."

"Be careful. Please."

"Wouldn't have it any other way, Sweet Cheeks." She scooted out of the way and laughed before he could grab her.

Watching her walk towards the office, he was reminded of what had almost happened last night. It had been awhile since he'd been with a woman but that didn't explain his reaction to her being so close. He'd wanted her so much his body physically hurt. He should be happy that the door slammed when it did. He really didn't need the complication of Evie right now.

~*~

Evie knew the best approach would be more direct with this one. Susan had been around seamen most of her life and wouldn't put up with a whiny, crying female. "Good morning." She said as she walked into the office.

"Hi ya. What can I do for you?" she asked with a heavy accent.

"I was hoping you could help me. I think my fiancé is cheating on me. I found a receipt for the shop. Can you tell me if you've seen him? It would have been last year."

"Men are bastards, ya know." She grabbed the photo and studied it. "Yeah, I remember him. Had all these demands about what kind of boat he wanted, nothing seemed good enough, then he brought the damn thing back damaged."

"What kind of damage?"

"One of the seats was practically ripped off. Not easy to do on my boats I can tell you that. He paid cash, including fixing everything."

"Did he have anyone with him?"

"Nope, going out or coming in. Can't tell you what he did during that time."

"Thank you for your time."

"No problem. Dump him, no man is worth it."

"Thanks, again."

Evie walked back out into the sunshine and toward Anthony. *Maybe, sometimes they are worth it.*

~*~

They stopped at a restaurant on the water. At a table overlooking the setting sun, they talked about things that had nothing to do with Jeremy. It was a nice change from all the darkness. Once they found out they both liked to quote movies they had a fun conversation trying to use only movie quotes.

Evie leaned back in her chair patting her stomach. "That was wonderful. Nothing like a good meal to make things seem brighter."

He shook his head. "Where do you put it all? I can't remember ever seeing a woman eat so much."

She shrugged. "I like food. I like to eat. I'm not going to be a female and just eat a little bit because I'm out with a man. If I'm hungry I eat, shouldn't matter who you're with."

There was a four-piece band playing music from the fifties in the corner. Evie turned to watch some older couples dance together on the small dance floor. She could remember her grandparents dancing together like that all the time. While her grandmother might be a bit wild, when she was married to her grandpa, Allen, it was one of the most romantic relationships she had ever seen.

"Would you like to dance?" Anthony asked.

She turned to him; sitting there in the candlelight with the vibrant colors of the sunset behind him. His white button-down shirt, open at the collar, and charcoal grey jacket looked dashing. "Yes, yes I would."

He stood up and offered his hand. She slid hers into his and felt the warmth seep through her. He led her through the tables to the dance floor. She was completely focused on him. He spun her around once before bringing her close to him. She wrapped her arm around his shoulder. His arm slid around her waist and he brought his other hand, with hers in it twisting them around so that the back of her hand was against his heart. She could feel the heat between them. They moved in time to the music across the dance floor, never taking their eyes off each other.

He led her in quick circles around the dance floor to the beat of the music. The rest of the room seemed to disappear until it was just the two of them. Stopping in the middle of the dance floor as the other couples danced and spun around them, he pulled her closer. She melted into him, needing to be close. He let go of her hand and moved it up to the side of her face.

"Evie, la mia belezza."

With her heart racing, she closed the distance between their lips. Their lips slid across each other's. She gripped his shoulders wanting him even closer. She could feel his fingers digging into her waist. She nipped at his lower lip and was rewarded with his mouth opening and his tongue coming out to meet hers.

They were jolted from behind as another coupled danced into them. "Sorry," they said as they danced on by.

Staring at Anthony, Evie wasn't sure what to do. She knew what she wanted to do. However, obviously, the dance floor wasn't the place to do it.

Holding his hand out to her he said, "Come on. Let's go home."

~*~

Unaware that Anthony and Evie were looking into his past, Jeremy laid back in bed casually looking over at the woman next to him. He'd never been with a woman as long as this one and he hated it. Not sure how much more he was going to be able to take, he tried to tune her out as she babbled on about some stupid author that she thought was the best thing ever.

He knew it was a calculated risk bringing her here, but he needed some refinement. He was tired of beer and pizza. It reminded him too much of his youth. Looking over the spread of food on the bed, he'd missed the finer things in life that was for sure.

When she started describing the fourth book he decided it was time for this to end. He knew that coming here was tempting fate. The police or Anthony could at any moment discover this place. He might as well leave them something to remind them of him. He casually picked up a fork and polished it on his shirt before turning towards her and stabbing it down into her gut, twisting, bending it down and pulling it out.

~*~

He dusted his hands off and surveyed his handiwork. Everything looked perfect. He couldn't wait for Anthony to find this, and he knew he would. It was just a matter of time. Turning the A/C down he walked out of the apartment and prepared to take a trip up north.

– CHAPTER FIVE –

Evie sighed behind the wheel. "Another Thursday, Yippee."

"Oh, come on, it's fun. We get to see what's new at the senior center and I get to play poker with the girls." Evelyne said.

"You see the girls all the time and you already know all the gossip. You're just there to watch the landscapers."

"Well, duh. Best part of my week and the only action I've been seeing lately."

"Thank goodness for that."

"You know you could use a little action. Maybe lighten you up a bit. You've been pretty testy lately."

Evie thought about her and Anthony's too brief of kiss last night. She was hoping when he said 'Let's go home' he meant something different than what it ended up being. He dropped her off then went into the cottage. Alone. She hadn't been able to get much sleep tossing and turning all night thinking about him.

"Did you hear what I said? Really girl, get your head out of the clouds."

"Sorry, what?"

"I asked how things went yesterday."

"Oh fine, we really didn't learn anything new. He's a neat freak, likes things a certain way and paid cash.""Well, maybe if you find where he is staying you can mess everything up and piss him off."

Shaking her head Evie noticed that there was a van following them. Since Evelyne liked to check the neighborhoods, to see what was new, on her way over to the senior center they weren't taking a direct route, yet this van seemed to keep finding them and following where they were going.

"That's strange."

"What honey?"

"Don't look, promise."

"Sure. I can do that."

"Don't turn around. But there seems to be a van following us." When she caught Evelyne starting to turn around, she hissed at her.

"Fine, but how am I supposed to describe it if you won't let me look. You know, it could be one of Noah's men."

"Why would they be following us?"

Evelyne shrugged. "I don't know, but you know how protective he is, maybe he just wants to make sure we are all safe."

Evie didn't think that was the case. Now she had to decide if she was going to say anything to Anthony or not about this. Trying to get a look at the license plate was proving to be more difficult than you would think. She was about to let her grandmother take a look when the driver turned onto another street and they never saw the van again.

~*~

Evie spent most of the day avoiding Anthony. Spending most of her time out of the house. This was unusual since typically she liked to face things head-on. After eating dinner at the diner in town so she wouldn't have to eat with him, she decided enough was enough. She went over and knocked on his door. Taking a deep breath, she entered after he said to come in.

He was sitting at the kitchen table with files spread out all over the place. She noticed a new poster on the wall. It had all the women listed with their information, the date they were murdered and pictures, thankfully of when they were alive. Walking over to it she was struck at how much they did resemble each other.

"That's strange," she said.

Getting up, he came to stand next to her. "What?"

"This." She pointed to the time between Lexi and Christina. "This was when you were in prison. So he didn't do any killing that whole time? Doesn't it seem strange, he was going about once a year up to that point? Then he is able to just quit for over five years? That doesn't make sense."

"Hmmm… you're right. I wonder how he could do that. He did tell Lexi that he had put himself in a self-imposed prison while I was locked up."

Turning to him she said, "Do you really think he could go that long? I hate to say it, but maybe there are other murders out there we know nothing about."

Running his hands over his face, he sighed and looked over at Evie. "I hope you're wrong. I really do."

"Me, too. Me, too. So what's the plan for tomorrow?"

She watched as he walked back over to the table and picked up a file. "I thought we could go talk to the ex-husband of the lady that was killed in the next town. He probably won't be able to tell us anything different than this police report says, but I figure it's worth a try. Here, you can read this report tonight."

"Thanks. I'll see you tomorrow then?"

"I'll come for you about ten in the morning."

Evie knew she was spending too much time with her grandmother; it was all she could do not to giggle like a school girl at his choice of words. "Great, see you then." She left him, quickly walking through the garden to the safety of her room, before laying on her bed and looking at the ceiling, giggling until tears started running down her face.

– CHAPTER SIX –

"**A**re you sure you want to be in on this?" Evie asked Anthony as they drove to Tom Cooper's home to talk to him about Christina's murder.

"I'm certainly not leaving it all up to you. Who knows what character you'd get into this time."

"Fine," she said while she crossed her arms.

Anthony was starting to get more and more nervous the more time he was apart from Evie. After their kiss the other night, he felt it would be better to take a step back. He didn't want her in harm's way, but he wanted her next to him at the same time. They still didn't have any idea where Jeremy was or if he was watching him right now. He looked in the rearview mirror, a habit he'd developed since getting out of prison and learning about Jeremy. Seeing nothing back there, he pulled into the driveway.

"Let me, at least, start things out. I'm sure he's seen photos of you and Jeremy, we don't want him to come out swinging."

"Fine," he said while he crossed his arms.

She gave him a little smirk at his imitation of her and walked up to the front door. After a brief discussion, she waved him over.

They sat down in a modest living room. Anthony looked around and saw pictures of two young children. He knew he wasn't directly responsible, but it still affected him. These children would grow up without a mother because of that sick bastard. "I'm sorry for your loss."

"Thank you. I've got to say it's kind of creepy sitting here looking at you knowing that someone is out there who killed Christina and looks just like you."

"It's strange for me, too. Is there anything you can tell us? Anything at all that might help us find him?"

"I'm sorry there really isn't much to tell. After the divorce, we weren't that close. I had primary custody of the kids. Christina liked to have a good time. This arrangement suited her. She'd been making some comments about meeting someone online that had a lot of money and was going to take care of her. But she never mentioned anything else."

"Did she happen to mention a screen name? Or at least which site she was on?" Evie asked. She had dug a notebook and pen out of her purse.

Tom sat there for a moment before he said, "No, no screen name. I think she was on *Finding Love* or something like that. Her typical screen name was *hottest momma*. I don't know if that will help."

"Thank you, it's something for us to look into. We won't take up any more of your time." Evie stood and started to walk to the door. She turned back around when Anthony called her name.

"Could you give us a few minutes alone?"

"Sure, I'll meet you in the car."

After she closed the door Anthony turned to Tom. "I cannot tell you how sorry I am. How are your children handling everything?"

Tom shrugged. "As good as can be expected. While she wasn't the best mom, hell, she wasn't around half of the time, she was still their mother. It's not easy with them hearing everything that happened. Besides there have been some added expenses we weren't planning on. But we'll get by, we always do."

"Thank you for taking the time to talk with us. Hopefully, we'll be able to catch this guy soon."

"I'm sorry to say this, but I've read what he's done, and I hope he doesn't make it out alive."

After the door closed, Anthony pulled out his phone and made a call to his lawyer. He set up a small trust fund for the children to help with their schooling and college. Feeling it was the least he could do to help, he walked back to the car with a little lighter step.

~*~

"Wow, are you reading any of this?" Evie asked Anthony as they sat at the kitchen table with a plate of fruit and cheese between them while working on laptops.

"Not really, just trying to see if we can find Christina."

"Seriously, you should read some of this. It's classic."

"Well, I figure we're kind of in a time crunch, so maybe it's more important to not get sidetracked."

"Party-pooper."

"Whatever it takes. Have you found anything useful that doesn't have to do with liking long walks on the beach?"

"Actually yes, it seems that on this site if you are in contact with someone it shows up on the sidebar. I'm hoping if we find Christina we can find Jeremy. She must have lied about her age or something because she's not coming up in this age bracket."

"Now, there's a surprise. Let's try going down to twenty-nine. Seems women love to say they're that age."

"I'll ignore that comment. I've also found that unless you delete your profile it stays up there. I found this woman who hasn't been active in three years. That's good news."

"Unless he deleted her profile after he killed her."

"Well, aren't you little Mr. Sunshine?"

"Can we please just continue?"

"Fine."

They worked in silence for another hour before Evie let out a whoop and stood up shaking her ass around the room.

"I take it you found something?"

"Yep, Sherlock, I sure did. Look here." She turned her laptop around and moved so that she stood next to him to point out the profile. "There she is. I was nervous, I couldn't click on it. This could be the break we're looking for."

Anthony slowly reached over and clicked it. They both leaned in closer. She was torn between burying her face in his neck and inhaling his intoxicating scent and or moving her head and scanning the screen for something that could help them. Responsibility won out.

"There." He tapped the screen. "There he is. Let's see what he has to say."

They scanned the profile of Jay Ellison. There wasn't any new information. Except the name.

Anthony turned towards her. "We never thought to do a search on a Jay Ellison. Maybe we can get more information."

Their faces were inches apart. She slowly blinked, trying to focus on his words and not his mesmerizing blue eyes. When she saw his pupils dilate, she knew he was feeling the same thing. Disappointment flowed through her when he blinked a few times then turned back to the screen.

Standing up she walked to the other side of the room. She went to focus on the maps, hoping something might come to her. Turning back around she said to him, "Maybe we should go interview people who had ties to the other murders."

Sitting back in the chair he crossed his arms across his chest. "You might have a good idea there."

"Not might, I *do* have a good idea. Look what we learned today. It's something, even if they can't give us much information, every little bit will help. Come on. Since we are on this coast I think we should start with Natalie. I know this will be the hardest for you, so we should get it over with first."

"You're right. But *I* will be doing this alone."

"Alone, what the hell are you talking about? I'm in this one hundred percent. *I* go with you."

He got up and walked over to her standing right in front of her trying to intimidate her. "No, you don't."

"You know I'll just book my own flight and be right behind you. So your choice is to let me do this on my own, or take me with you. Your pick, but I *am* going. Now move out of my way, I've got a flight to book."

She tried to push past him but he just pinned her to the wall. In a voice which was too calm and soft compared to the fire in his eyes, he said, "No, you're not going."

"What are you going to do? Tie me to the bed?" The image flashed through her mind before she could stop it.

"Don't tempt me. I'm sure your grandmother would be on my side."

"Actually you'd be wrong buddy, she's behind me. She might not like it, but she supports me. You might as well give in now. I really don't want to be up all night fighting." Her breathing started to increase.

"Then give in and we won't."

"I *never* give in."

"We'll just have to see about that." He pressed his body into hers and devoured her mouth. Grabbing her ass, he hoisted her up so she was pinned to the wall.

With his hands occupied, she took the opportunity to dive her hands into his hair, grabbing hard and pulling his head back from her swollen lips. She could see the passion in his hooded eyes. Yanking him back to her lips, they continued their battle of wills with their kisses. She wanted his hands free, wanted to feel them all over her body. She wrapped her legs around his waist. She didn't have to wait long before she felt his hands on her breasts, squeezing and pinching. Letting out a primal moan, she tightened her legs around him, trying to get closer to the hardness she could feel between them.

Moving away from the wall he spun around and laid her on the table pushing everything out of the way, his lips never leaving hers. Her touches became frantic with the thought of having him inside of her. The blood pumped so fast in her veins, her ears rang.

The ringing wasn't just in her ears and she whimpered when he pulled his lips from hers and glared over at the phone. With a curse, he left her and answered the call. His eyes burned with passion as he talked to whoever was on the other end of the call.

Hearing the frustration in his voice, she knew it wasn't going to be a quick phone call. Getting up from the table she grabbed her laptop and started to walk out the door. She continued to leave even when she heard him say "Hold on."

She was whipped back around and his lips came down hard on hers. "I'm sorry; I've got to take this. Book us both a flight for the first available they have."

Not trusting her voice, she just nodded and walked out into the cool night air.

– CHAPTER SEVEN –

E vie sighed. *It's going to be a long day*. She had to take her grandmother to the doctor's office to see how she was doing. Unfortunately, it was a new doctor, a young doctor, a good looking doctor.

Having spent the good part of the past hour trying to convince her that she didn't need to take her clothes off for the exam they were finally on their way back home. Evie was pretty sure after how quickly the doctor left the room there was going to be a note on her grandmother's file that he never wanted to see her again.

When they pulled into the driveway, Evie saw that Anthony's car was still there. Knowing what was coming next, she took a deep breath and turned to her grandmother. "We've got to talk. Let's sit on the front porch."

"This can't be good. If this has anything to do with the pictures, I can explain."

Closing her eyes and leaning her head back against the headrest Evie said, "What pictures?"

Evelyne tried to look bashful, "Oh, nothing. We don't need to worry about it."

Knowing she would probably hate herself later, Evie decided to wait until later to deal with it. Or better yet, let her brother Jackson deal with it. He should be here within the next few hours. They walked towards the porch and sat down.

"Okay, Grams, I'll let this go." Seeing her hopeful expression Evie added, "For now."

"Great. Now what did you want to talk about?"

"Do you want something to drink? Maybe some lemonade would be nice." Evie started to get up to go inside to get some when Evelyne grabbed her hand and pulled her back down on the seat.

"Spill."

"When does that ever work with you?"

"Never, but you started this."

"True. Fine. Anthony and I are going to England. Before you say anything you know we've been interviewing people who had contact with Jeremy last year. We did get some more information that wasn't in the police reports. Most of it not that useful, but one piece was good. He had an online profile using the name Jay Ellison. We are looking into that, but we decided that talking to other people might give us something helpful."

When her grandmother hadn't said anything, Evie glanced at her out of the corner of her eye. She stared straight ahead.

"Say something."

Slowly, she turned her head towards Evie. "I don't like it." Before Evie could open her mouth to protest, Evelyne continued, "But I can see that it might be a good idea. Are you sure you have to go? Of course you do, who am I talking to? You'll be careful, right?"

Evie leaned over and hugged her. "I'll be more careful than usual, how's that?" At Evelyne's soft chuckle, Evie closed her eyes and enjoyed being close to her.

"What about your business? Can you take more time off?"

"Yes, I've been in daily contact with Jesse, things are running fine without me. Almost too well. I feel like I'm not needed anymore. It's a little sad, but it's good to know that I can take the time to do this."

"I do have another question, what's going on between you and Anthony?"

"Nothing. Nothing at all."

"Is that a good or bad thing? You've been spending a lot of time with him, and now traveling. Well, things could happen."

"Yes they could, but they won't. I don't think either one of us wants that kind of distraction right now. Besides, I really don't want to be in Jeremy's cross-hairs by having a relationship with Anthony."

"If Jeremy wasn't in the picture?"

"Well he is, so we don't have to think about it."

"Hmmm…"

"Hmmm what?"

"Nothing. How long do you think you'll be gone and who is going to stay with me?"

"I'm not sure. We've got an open-ended return ticket. Depending on what we find, we might have to travel somewhere else. We could be gone a couple of weeks. I'm really not sure. As to who is going to stay with you, I came up with the perfect solution."

"Is he young and hot and willing to give me sponge-baths?"

Evie chuckled. "Well, he is young, some people think he's hot and just ew gross." At her grandmother's confused look, she continued. "It's Jackson. I managed to guilt him into stop roaming around the world to come here."

"Well, shit. He's not going to let me have any fun."

"You got that right. I should've made him come here earlier."

"Really Evie, I thought you loved me." Evelyne tried to look wounded.

"You can't fool me, old lady. You'll just have to devise new ways to cause trouble with him around. I'm sure you're up to the task."

"That I am, that I am."

~*~

"Lock your daughters up, Jackson is back in town!" A voice boomed from the front of the house.

Evie ran to him and jumped in his arms. "How's the best brother in the whole wide world? It's so good to see you! I've missed you."

He spun her around, making her giggle, before putting her down. "I'm great. Wondering what I'm going to do for the next few weeks, but I'm sure something will come up. Now tell me what's going on."

They sat around together while the ladies filled him in. There were some raised voices as they fought about what Evie was going to do, but finally he calmed down and said he was going to talk to Anthony, alone.

Evie bit her lip in worry and watched out the kitchen window to the cottage. She wished she could hear what they were talking about. Finally her brother came out and walked back into the house.

"Well."

"Well what?"

"What did you guys talk about?"

"You."

"What about me?"

"Stuff."

"Gee Jack, could you stop talking so much? I can't get a word in edgewise."

He put her in a headlock and dragged her to the couch where they both sat down. "We just talked man to man. Made sure we understood where the other stands."

"And where do you stand?"

"We both want this bastard caught, that's all you need to worry your pretty, little head about." He reached over and messed up her hair.

"Come on. Quit being such an ass. Details, I need details."

"Why is what we talked about so important to you?" He squinted at her.

Hoping she hadn't given anything away about her attraction to Anthony, she tried to shrug it off. "Well, we're going to be working together a lot. In close quarters. I just wanted to make sure you weren't a huge jerk that might make that uncomfortable."

He looked at her for a long time. Trying not to squirm under his scrutiny, she held his gaze.

Patting her on the head he stood up. "That had better be it. He's had a rough time. I'd hate to have to kick his ass."

After he walked out of the room Evie let the breath she had been holding out. She was glad they were going to be leaving on their trip soon. Hiding her feelings from her brother had never been something she'd been able to do.

Evie knocked on the cottage door after receiving an urgent text from Anthony. She didn't know why he didn't just come over to the house but she felt it had something to do with her brother.

"Come in."

Entering the cottage, she stopped at the sight of him in the bedroom. He had a towel on and there were drops of water falling down his skin. She had felt his muscles, she knew he had them, but seeing them was something different. Taking a step towards him before she could stop herself, she almost gave in to running her hands all over him and licking him dry.

Turning towards her he smiled. "I didn't think you'd be here so quick. Sorry, let me get dressed. I'll be right out."

Don't hurry on my account. Glad he didn't close the door, she sat down and watched out of the corner of her eye as his towel dropped and she was treated to one of the finest asses she'd ever seen. *I bet I could bounce a quarter on that. Shit, I'm getting as bad as my grandmother.*

All too quickly he was dressed and in the living room sitting down next to her on the couch. "I've got some news about Jay Ellison."

"Really? That was quick. What have you got?"

"We've found two properties that have the owners as Jay Ellison. One, we think, is the home he grew up in. The other is a condo in New York that was purchased by a Jay Ellison ten years ago."

"That can't be much, I'm sure there are thousands of Jay Ellison's in the country."

"True, but this one happens to have been left vacant and a property management company had been hired to oversee things for the past six years."

"Ok, well, that could be a coincidence."

"True, but then there's this." He showed her his phone. On it there was a directory of owners along with pictures.

"Well, hot damn. When do we leave?"

"How fast can you be packed?"

"Give me half an hour."

"I'll be waiting."

Evie ran out of the cottage and up to her room. Since they were going to be leaving in two days from Boston to London she decided to pack enough clothes for a week in case they weren't able to make it back here before their flight left.

Sitting down on the bed she took a look around her room that she'd stayed in since she was a child, somehow knowing that when she returned, things would be different.

– CHAPTER EIGHT –

On the sidewalk outside of Jeremy's building Evie turned to Anthony. "Let me do the talking. I think it will work better if I take point on this one."

"Is it even worth my energy to argue?"

"Nope, come on. Let's see what we can find out." She turned to make sure he was following her when she opened the door.

They crossed to the desk. Evie was thankful it was a middle aged man. She gave him a huge smile while she checked out his nametag. "Hi Cal, I was hoping you'd be able to help us."

"Sure, what can I do for you?" He stood up a little straighter.

She could tell by the way he looked at her and Anthony that he was confused and recognized him. She wanted to draw his attention back to her and not have it focused on Anthony too long.

"I'm Mr. Ellison's nurse. I'm not sure if you are aware of it, but he was in an accident and he is having a bit of a problem with his memory."

"Oh, I'm sorry to hear that. I was under the impression when you were here last week that you'd be around more. I was wondering what happened."

Evie's gut clutched as she thought of how close they were to finding him. Maybe he would even come home while they were there. "Lucky for him the accident wasn't too bad except for the nasty bump on the head that has messed with his memory."

"What can I help you with?"

"Well, it's like this, he's lost his keys and wallet, the only way we knew who he was or where he lived was from the registration on his car. So you see, he has no way to get into his condo. Is there any way you could let us in?" She thought about batting her eyelashes but decided that might be a bit overboard.

Cal rubbed his hand along the back of his neck. "Well, it's kind of against company policy. I mean I do recognize him, so I guess it would be ok, right?" He looked at them with a hopeful expression like he was looking for validation in his thinking.

Evie rubbed the back of his hand that was resting on the desk. "Of course it would, and you would be helping him. We're hoping that having him spend some time around his things will help trigger his memory."

"Ok, but can we just keep this between us? I really need this job."

She felt a pang of guilt at lying to this nice man, but lives were at stake. They had to find Jeremy. "Not a problem."

Cal sighed in relief and gave them a key. "We always have spares around for the owners. Here you go."

"Thanks Cal, you're a real sweetheart." She turned and grabbed Anthony by the elbow and steered him towards the elevator. She could tell that she was squeezing too hard when he reached up and pried her fingers from him. "Sorry," she whispered.

They didn't say a word to each other as they rode the elevator up. They had talked about the fact this building could have cameras all around. The only place they would be free to talk would be in the enemy's lair.

~*~

Anthony shook his head as he watched Evie stride boldly into Jeremy's condo and dance around. Casually he wiped the doorknob clean with the sleeve of his jacket and pulled a couple of gloves out of his pocket and put them on.

"Did you see that? Did you fucking see that? Easier than taking candy from a baby. Damn I'm good." She smacked her ass and spun around.

"If you're done, maybe we could search the place?"

"Party-pooper. Fine, have it your way. Why is it so cold in here? It's like a morgue." She stopped and stared at him her eyes going wide. "No."

"It seems with Jeremy you never know. Maybe you should stay here while I look around."

"No way, we stick together."

"Think about it before you become the Queen of Stubborn. We don't know what we will find. If you search out here, I'll look around and make sure there aren't any surprises hiding. We kill two birds with one stone and get out of here quicker."

"Oh, no way. Haven't you seen any horror movies? When you split up is when someone gets killed. Nope, we do this together."

"Is that the only way I can get you to shut up?"

"Yep."

"Fine. I think you're worse than your grandmother."

"I'll take that as a compliment. Now, let's move it."

They walked down a short hallway opening up doors to a closet and bathroom. Nothing seemed out of the ordinary. He wanted to laugh at how she gripped his arm and held her breath with every door they opened. When they got to the last door, they looked at each other.

"You can always go back."

"No, no I can't."

"Here goes."

Slowly opening the door, his breath whooshed out of his lungs. He shook his head hoping that the image that he saw really wasn't there. Vaguely he could hear Evie's breathing beside him become rapid. There, spread out naked on the bed, was the body of a dead woman. Her torso had been cut open and her entrails were pulled out and forks jammed through them attaching them to other parts of her body. Some reached her eyes where forks were buried in each of them. Blood soaked into the white sheets and down the side leaving a dried puddle on the floor.

Her fingers were bent back at odd angles and her jaw was pried open and her mouth was stuffed with summer sausage. Above her, on the wall, was a message written in blood:

Who's next?

"Oh my god, oh my god, oh my god. Anthony, we've got to get out of here." Her voice raised in pitch with every word she said.

Anthony grabbed her and hauled her out of the room closing the door behind him. She kept saying the same thing over and over. He knew that he had to calm her down before she started screaming. He did the first thing that came to his mind and kissed her hard wrapping his arms around her. Feeling her that close to him was his undoing. He moved one hand up to grasp the back of her head and tangle his fingers in her hair. His fingers dug into her waist wanting more. He felt her melt against him for a moment before coming back to her senses and pushing him away.

"What in the hell are you doing? There's a dead woman in the next room."

"I had to do something to get you to calm down before you started screaming so loud the whole building would be breaking down the door."

"So the only reason you kissed me was to calm me down? Thanks, buddy."

"Now you're pissed because I kissed you to calm you down? A second ago it was because I kissed you in the first place. Which one is it?"

"Fuck, I don't know. I can't think. What should we do?" She spun around in circles her eyes looking everywhere.

"Get out of here. This could be another set up; the cops could be on their way."

"But we haven't searched the rest of the place. There could be something important here." She stopped and gripped his hands.

He was trying to block out the image that was in his mind, but he knew it would be there for a long time. He wanted to get as far away from the horror in the other room. Wanting to get both of them out of there, but knowing she had a point, he had to go back in that room. In his mind, if Jeremy had left anything it would have been in there, knowing that either Anthony would leave without finding it or if he did go back in there, it would torture him even more.

"Fine, but be quick. You search out here, I'll go back in."

Her eyes became wide. "You... you mean to go back in there?"

"I have no choice." He turned and strode away from her and back into hell.

~*~

As an alarm sounded on his computer, a sick smile spread across Jeremy's face. They'd found his place in New York. Picking up the phone, he made a phone call then sat back to watch the chaos unfold.

~*~

Taking a moment to get herself under control she could do nothing but stare blindly out the window. If she didn't get it under control, she would break everything she could get her hands on. Shaking her head to clear it, she turned around to face the room to decide where to start.

There wasn't much to search out here, so it didn't take her long to find the letter on the kitchen counter with Anthony's name on it. She chewed on her lower lip wondering if she should interrupt him or just let him finish. They really needed all the information they could get. With the letter in her hands her fingers itched to open it, she stood in the middle of living room staring at the closed bedroom door willing it to open. When it finally did, the air whooshed out of her lungs.

It looked like his skin was stretched tight across his face and his eyes held a haunted look she wasn't sure would ever go away. Walking to him she held her arms open and he collapsed into them. She could feel the shivers run through his body.

"That poor woman, she didn't deserve that." His voice was muffled as his face was buried in her neck.

"No, she didn't. None of them did. That's why we've got to catch that bastard. Did you find anything?"

"Nothing, everything was cleaned out. There was nothing of his in there. What did you find?"

She pulled away from him and handed him the letter. She watched as with shaking fingers he opened it. Moving around to stand behind him she raised up on her toes to read over his shoulder.

My dearest Anthony,

Welcome to my home. Feel free to kick back and stay awhile.

I hope you enjoy my little gift. I must admit, I wasn't planning on giving it to you so soon, however, situations change, and well, quite frankly I couldn't stand the bitch any longer. Not up to my usual standards either, but what can I say, I let my emotions get ahold of me. Although it was quite a bit of fun to rip open her stomach and allow her guts to run through my fingers. It caused me a lot of glee to be able to see how far I could stretch them before using a fork to pin them to different parts of her body.

Since I know everything about you, I'd thought I'd give you a little something of me. Hear this, know this, I will never give up until everything you love has been taken from you. Until you are left in a puddle of grief on the side of the road wallowing in your own self-pity. Even then, that won't be enough. I want you to suffer through a millennia of pain with no end in sight.

Good day, I'll be watching,

Jeremy

P.S. I've called the police, they should be there any moment.

She could feel the heat radiating off of him and started to back away. He crumpled the paper in his hand and punched the wall with the other. Before he could scream in rage, she went up and covered his mouth. He looked at her with so much hatred in his eyes, it took everything she had not to run. "I know, but you've got to get ahold of yourself. We have to get out of here."

They both froze as they heard sirens in the distance. He grabbed her hand and they ran out the door. He stopped briefly to call for the elevator. As soon as it opened, he pushed all the buttons. They ran towards the stairs and flew down them. From inside the stairwell, they couldn't hear if the sirens were getting closer or not. They might not even be coming here but they couldn't take the chance.

Bursting out into the afternoon sun, they looked up and down the alley. Not seeing anything, they walked towards the street to get lost in the crowd never turning around when they heard the cars screech to a halt in front of the building they just came out of.

~*~

Once the door was closed and they were safely in their hotel room Evie pulled the wig off of her head and dropped it on the floor. She crossed to a chair and sat heavily in it. Her hands were still shaking and she couldn't get warm.

Looking up at him with huge eyes she could feel the tears start to build. Saying nothing he walked over to the bed and pulled the covers back. He walked back to the bathroom and turned the light on and the one by the bed off. When he took his shoes off, she still didn't know what he was doing. He walked over and picked her up then carried her to the bed.

"What are you doing?"

"Shhh… come on, lay down. We've both had a lot to deal with."

Not having the energy to fight with him she let him tuck her in. She didn't even protest when he climbed in behind her and pulled her close. Letting his heat seep into her, she closed her eyes and fell asleep feeling safe in his arms for the first time in hours.

– CHAPTER NINE –

Evie woke up slowly with a hard body behind her. Opening her eyes, she was torn between staying in his warm embrace or getting up and starting to dwell on what had happened yesterday. Deciding that she could just as easily stay in his arms as dwell on the murdered woman, she stayed where she was.

What must she have gone through? The pain she must have suffered at the hands of madman. She wondered if she had any family or friends that would miss her. She was someone's daughter, someone's first love, maybe even someone's mother. To have all that taken away was just so sad.

Tears started falling down her cheeks. How could someone do that to another human being? She knew everything that happened to Lexi, both times, along with the other women. For someone to continue to do that, they must be seriously fucked up. Knowing he would keep killing until he was captured did nothing to help Evie calm down.

The arms that were around her squeezed and pulled her closer. She held her breath not sure if he was awake. Torn between knowing they had to get up and get out of here and wanting to spend all day close to him, she did nothing.

"How long do you think we can hide out here?" he mumbled in her ear.

"I'd give it a couple of days before having to do the right thing surfaces."

"It's so warm and comfortable lying here with you, I don't ever want to leave."

Evie shivered, at a loss for what to do or say. This was a first for her and she didn't like the feeling one bit.

"Ahhh... finally I've found a way to keep you quiet. Maybe I should try something else." With one arm holding her tight against him, he used his other hand to move the hair away from her neck. He nipped and licked the side of her neck as his free hand roamed down the length of her body.

"Yes, I think this is perfect. You taste so good." He raised her arm and entwined it with his, breathing softly against the inside of her elbow. "My imagination runs wild as to what the rest of you tastes like." His tongue licked her wrist.

She couldn't stand it any longer. Moaning, she turned in his arms and moved her leg over his. With the heel of her foot, pulled him closer, so that his hardness was tight against her.

Pushing her shoulder back so she was arched, he dipped his head and bit her nipple through her clothes. Grinding against each other he pulled her shirt up roughly, forcing her bra out of the way. Without hesitation, he sucked on her nipple.

Letting out a cry of pleasure, she unbuttoned his pants. She had just reached her hand in and was about to wrap her hand around him, when a knock sounded on the door.

"Seriously?" She yelled turning on her back.

"Housekeeping."

"Not now." He bellowed pulling her back towards him.

"Check out is now. You must leave."

"Shit. Fuck. Damn. Why does this keep happening to us?"

He rolled away from her adjusting himself as he stood up. "One of these days there won't be an interruption."

"Can't be soon enough for me."

Sending her a lopsided grin he said, "Me either, me either."

~*~

Jeremy watched the video over and over from his hotel room in Boston. Seeing them in one of his homes was thrilling. He had edited the video so that it showed his favorite parts only. Watching them creep down the hall, the look of terror on her face wondering what they would find. Then finally the coup de grâce when they opened the door to the bedroom.

He froze the frame so that he could look at them. A laugh escaped his lips, he couldn't keep it in. Gently stroking the screen, he knew this was an image he'd keep in his mind forever.

Cocking his head to the side, he took a closer look at the woman with Anthony. Evie Taylor, Lexi's best friend, and it would appear Anthony's new woman. Not his usual woman, not their typical women, but there was something about her. He could almost feel her fear through the screen. Wanting more, he began to make plans.

Anthony had mixed feelings about coming home. Torn between wishing his parents were still alive and being thankful they weren't put through everything that had happened the past eight years.

Looking down at Evie who rested her head on his shoulder in the car, he wondered what they would have thought about her. Chuckling to himself he knew his mother would have gotten a kick out of her and his father would have loved to have a sparring partner with her.

They had plenty of time to drive from New York to Boston to catch their flight. He could tell by the way she kept playing with the strap on her bag she was nervous someone was going to stop them going through security, but when no one did he could see her visibly relax. Thinking she would fall asleep as soon as they were in the air because of all the stress he was surprised she stayed awake for the whole flight. Well, he assumed she did since every time he woke up because he was worried about her she was sitting there staring out the window. However, since he didn't get much sleep the night before he was unable to keep his eyes open or even comfort her.

Pulling up in front of the home generations of Maldonos had owned, Anthony filled with a feeling that this was where he needed to be. He made sure Evie wouldn't tip over when she was no longer propped up by him he got out of the car. Going around to her side while the driver got their suitcases, he reached in and grabbed her. She fit so perfectly in his arms and when she wrapped her arms around his neck, he just wanted to take her up to his bedroom and spend the day making love to her. He liked having her here with him. It was nice to have someone stand by his side when he'd been alone for so long.

Laying her down on the bed in the guest room, he smiled when she whimpered as his arms released her. He knew that she wanted him just as much as he wanted her. He wanted to get some work done but didn't want to be too far away when she woke back up, so he got his files and sat down in the sitting area of her room. Anthony got to work planning what they would be doing while here.

~*~

Evie opened her eyes to the richest room she had ever seen. It was old world meets new. Classic antiques next to modern conveniences, yet somehow it worked. She sat up but stopped mid-stretch when she noticed Anthony watching her. "Hey."

"Good morning. Sleep well?"

"Yes, is it really morning? Did I sleep for the past twenty-four hours?" Her body didn't feel like it had been in bed that long.

"No, it's just after noon. I'm glad you are awake, I didn't want you to sleep too much, jet-lag and all that."

"Thanks. So, why are you here?"

"I live here."

"Ha-ha, no I mean here with me in this room."

"Since you were asleep when we got here I was worried you wouldn't know where you were when you woke up."

"Thanks, but it couldn't have been much fun for you."

"On the contrary, watching you sleep was an enlightening experience."

Not sure how to take his words she decided not to comment and change the subject. "What are all those files for?"

"Just going over the information on Jeremy again and coming up with a plan. I feel like I should have this memorized by now."

"Would you like to fill me in on the plan?"

"Well, you don't have to worry about dressing up and acting. Sorry to disappoint."

Sticking her tongue out, she got out of bed and walked over to her suitcases. "I need to get cleaned up. What are the plans for the rest of the day?"

"How are you feeling?"

"Fine, why?"

"Because I'd like to go out to Sutton's country manor today. It's only a couple of hours drive but it would give us a head start."

Evie had never been to London before and was hoping for a little bit of sight-seeing, but it appeared that she was going to have to settle for seeing it from the car. "I'm fine. Can I have about a half hour or so? And maybe some coffee?"

"Sure, I'll see to that. The kitchen is two levels down."

"Thanks, I'll be there."

At the door he turned back around. "Do you want me to wash your back?"

Shivering at the thought she shook her head. "Not if you want to get out to the Sutton's in the next day or so."

"Right, well then, I'd better go."

Standing there with a shirt clutched to her chest, she wondered how she'd had the strength to turn him down.

~*~

The trip out to the Sutton's went too quick for Evie. She was awed and amazed at how different everything looked. She loved the architecture, loved the look of the buildings which were hundreds of years old. You could almost feel the history radiating off of them.

"*This* is their *country* home?" She leaned forward to get a look at a home which was bigger than anything she'd ever seen. "I'm going to get lost in there."

"I guess this isn't the time to tell you that this is the smallest of the homes they own."

"Nope, I don't want to hear about it. What am I going to say to them? We couldn't have anything in common."

"You have more than you know. Just relax and be yourself."

"What if I curse in front of them? Shit, I just know I will. See?"

Laughing, he reached over and grabbed her hand. "You'll be fine."

As they pulled up, the front the door opened and an older couple came out to meet them.

Evie turned to Anthony. "You know I am completely out of my element. You are going to have to help me not make a complete fool out of myself. Please."

He stopped the car and turned to her, framing her face with his hands. "Breathe, la mia belezza. Everything will be fine. I'll be right here with you." He gave her a light kiss before opening the door and getting out.

Evie got out of the car more slowly after Anthony had opened it for her and followed him to where he was giving the lady a big hug. With his arm still around her he turned around to introduce them. "Evie, this is Eugene and Louise Sutton. Gene and Lou, this is Evie Taylor."

"Nice to meet you both. Thank you so much for allowing us to come out here."

Lou waved her off. "It's no problem, love, we miss having younger company. Besides we haven't seen this scamp in a long time." She slapped his arm. "Way too long."

Grinning he said, "Not my fault. But I'm here now, even though we can't stay too long."

"I'll take what I can get. Now why don't we get you two settled? Dinner is almost ready. Come, come." Lou turned and walked back into the house. Evie started to follow but stopped when Anthony and Gene didn't immediately follow.

"Don't worry, I'll be right there. I just need a moment."

~*~

Anthony hated leaving her alone even for a minute, but he wanted a quick private word with Gene. "Is she going to be fine with this?"

"As fine as anyone can be. We never stop hurting or remembering. It's just the times in between, when the pain is unbearable, stretches a bit as the years go by. But they aren't as frequent."

"I can't believe everything that has happened. I've always felt bad for what happened to Natalie, but now, I feel it's all my fault she was killed."

"Son, you can't think like that. It's not your fault. This individual is sick and twisted; he was bound to focus on someone. Bad luck it was you."

"I've got to catch him Gene, this can't go on."

"No, it can't. Now let's go in before that young lady wonders what happened to you."

Evie spun in circles looking around the huge room. It was filled floor to ceiling, two levels, with books. She felt like a kid in a candy store. Rushing to one of the shelves she didn't notice Anthony and Gene walk into the room. Carefully taking a book out, she laid her hand over the cover and closed her eyes. Opening the book, she moved it up to her face and breathed in deeply. She jumped when Gene started talking.

"There's nothing like the smell of a book is there?"

"No, not at all. Look at all of this!" She spread her arms wide. "I could live in this room for years and never come out."

When Evie's sparkling eyes met Anthony's, it seemed like everything else faded into the background and it was just the two of them. Unspoken desire flowed between them. She took an involuntary step toward him, but the spell was broken when Lou touched her on the arm.

"Come on, dear, I'll show you your room and then we can sit down to eat. Anthony, I've put you in the old room you used to stay in."

"Thank you. If you don't mind I'd like to make sure Evie is close by me. You completely understand why, of course."

"We understand more than you think." Lou said with a soft smile. "I've already put her in the room next to yours."

"Wonderful, we'll get changed for dinner and be down," Anthony said.

Walking into her huge room Evie was once again awed. She was scared to touch anything, but she couldn't resist running her hand over the old wood. There was such history all around her. As soon as she was alone, she started opening doors to see what was behind them. She stood for a few minutes staring at the unbelievably luxurious bathroom before moving onto the last door.

Opening the door she gasped. Standing there was a naked Anthony.

"Oops." Quickly she closed the door and leaned back on it. "Oh holy hell am I in trouble." Hearing his laugh from the other room, she kicked the door in frustration. Immediately she dropped to the floor and checked to make sure she didn't damage anything. Seeing everything was fine, she sat down and stared, knowing he was naked behind the door, wanting to open it and get lost in him.

~*~

Jeremy smiled as he got in the car and sped away from Anthony's home in London. Sometimes it was just too easy.

~*~

"Are you sure you want to do this?" Evie asked as they entered the attic.

"No, I really don't. But if we learn something new, then it will all be worth it."

Stopping she looked around. "There is so much up here. It's huge!"

"Yes, hundreds of years' worth of history up here. Lucky they are organized. The deeper you go, the further you go back in time."

"OK, where do we start?"

"Just right here. They said they boxed up all of Natalie's stuff and it should be here."

"What's first?"

"With the first box we can get to. Here you go." He hands her a box and she sits down on the floor.

They started going through them. Most were clothes and books and they were easy to sort. By the time that was done, they ended up with a couple dozen boxes to go through.

"Is there any electricity up here?"

"Of course."

"Okay, is there a plug around here? I've got an old computer that might have some information on it. It's a long shot after all of this time, but there might be something."

"Yeah, hold on, there should be one around here somewhere." He started moving boxes to look at the wall. "You know you could just take it downstairs."

Batting her eyes at him she said, "Yes, but then I wouldn't be able to spend time with you."

Giving her a look of disbelief, she just giggled at him. "Fine, you know we can finish looking through these boxes and take the computer down later."

"Great idea."

"Tsk, tsk... sarcasm Anthony? I never would have expected that from you."

Turning towards her, he leaned up against the wall and crossed his arms over his chest. "Do you really want to go there?"

Stalking towards him she stopped, almost touching him. "You know I want to go there." She watched his pupils dilate.

"Come here." He growled.

With one quick movement, he had her wrapped in his arms. He brought his lips to hers, crushing them with his passion. Her arms wrapped tightly around his neck, her hands weaving through his hair, holding him to her.

As their tongues battled, he grabbed her ass and pulled her in closer. Moaning, she could feel his hardness pressed up against her. She slid her hands down until she found the bottom of his shirt. Lifting it upwards, she felt him shiver as her hand skimmed up his chest.

Pulling his lips from her, he nipped and kissed his way down her neck.

"I've never wanted someone as much as I've wanted you," he whispered. "What kind of spell have you put on me? You're in my thoughts all the time. I can taste you in my sleep."

His lips captured hers again. Shivering at his words, she was completely lost in the moment until she heard someone clear their throat.

"Sorry to interrupt, but lunch is ready." Louise said with a laugh in her voice.

Evie buried her face, which was beet red, in Anthony's chest. His arms came around her to hold her tight.

"Thanks, Lou. We'll be down in a moment."

"Should I time you?"

"Louise…"

Lou laughed as she walked out of the attic.

"Come on, la mia belezza, let's go eat."

"I can't face her." She mumbled into his chest feeling the rumble of his laugh.

"Come on, she hasn't gotten to her age without seeing people kiss before."

"You come on. The rate we were going, we'd have been naked in five minutes."

"Don't remind me. Let's grab something to eat and get this over with."

"I assume you are talking about going through everything and not jumping each other."

"Yes, Evie."

"Damn, I was afraid of that." She wanted him so badly she could barely see straight. One of these days they weren't going to be interrupted.

~*~

After spending all day going through the boxes and looking through Natalie's computer, they were unable to find anything new. Anthony was frustrated. After finding little things, at least, he was hoping to find something bigger here. It seemed like it was a wasted trip.

Not completely wasted though, he was able to spend some time with people he felt were an extension of his family. They were getting older and Anthony made a note to make sure he came back more often to visit them.

When they were saying good-bye for the trip back to London the next morning, he held onto Lou for a while. She was like another mom to him.

"She's pretty special, Anthony," Lou whispered.

"I know. I think Natalie would have liked her."

"Oh, she would have loved her. It does my heart good to see you with someone after all this time."

"We really aren't 'together.'"

"Could have fooled me. Remember, I'm the one who found you two in the attic." She pulled back and framed his face with her hands. "Don't waste this chance on fears of the past or what may come. Grab it, grab *her,* with both hands and never let go. Do you hear me? Never. Let. Go. Life is too short."

Pulling her back into a hug he rested his head on top of hers. "I know Lou, I know."

"Now, off you go. Have fun, go a little crazy."

Making sure Evie was settled into the car, he walked around to the driver's side where Gene waited for him.

After a brief man-hug, Gene said to him. "Find that bastard. Find him and make sure he pays for what he did to my little girl and all the other women and everything he's taken from you."

"That's the plan, sir."

"Make sure you keep that girl of yours safe."

Anthony turned around to see her talking quietly to Lou through the open window. The thought of Jeremy ever laying a hand on Evie made his heart contract in his chest. "That is my top priority."

"Good boy, now drive safe."

~*~

The ride back to London was uneventful and they sat in a combatable silence. Anthony enjoyed seeing the excitement Evie had for history. He took the long way around London so she had a chance to see more of it. Feeling bad this was such a short trip and she wasn't able to visit any historic sights, he vowed he would bring her back sometime when they could spend time wandering around.

They had just walked in when the butler came up to them. "Mr. Maldono, I wasn't expecting you until later today. I hope the files you came back for were of use."

Anthony and Evie looked at each other before he said. "What files? What are you talking about?" His stomach dropped.

"A couple of hours after you and Miss Taylor left you came back saying you forgot something and had to get it. You went up to your room and came back down a few minutes later with the files."

"Shit." Anthony ran upstairs to his room with Evie on his heels. "Stay back." He yelled over his shoulder at her.

"Like hell."

Skidding to a stop in front of his room he took a deep breath. Unsure of what would be behind the door. He felt Evie's hand on his back and knew he had to open the door.

Opening the door slowly he let his breath out. There was nothing out of the ordinary. They both walked in and looked around. Anthony walked over to his desk. His file on Jeremy was gone, including all of his thoughts and notes on the case. Sitting down in the chair feeling defeated, he was pissed off at having to recreate everything.

"Anthony."

Hearing the waiver in her voice he jumped out of the chair and went to her. She pointed to an envelope on the bed with his name on it. He reached over and opened it.

Dearest Anthony,

I hope this letter finds you well. It has been so much fun tracking you. I'm surprised at how predicable you've become. Really you need to step up your game if you want to catch me.

I noticed you found my gift. It was so much fun leaving her for you. I knew at some point you'd find that property and go there. Did it excite you? Seeing what I left for you? It excited me. I came all over her dead and rotting body. Something new for me, but I quite liked it.

You've got a lovely home here. Did you know over ten years ago I fucked one of your parent's maids? She thought she was fucking you, but hey, you can't win them all. It was my first time in your home. Sadly, she had to go missing.

Before I left I was able to go through the house and found many interesting things. Including the vehicles. Did you know one of my many odd jobs before I found my calling was at a mechanics shop? No? Well, it was. You learn a lot of fun things you can do to a vehicle and no one will know you tampered with it, if the damage is great enough.

Yes, I knew you might have decided to go with your parents that day, but I took a chance and it paid off. It was just them, a busy street and a horrific crash. My only regret was that I wasn't there to see it. At least, there were enough pictures.

Take care, Anthony. I'm closer than you think.
Jeremy

Anthony sat down hard on the bed. Jeremy had killed his parents. All this time they thought it was an accident. Looking up at Evie, he saw the tears streaming down her face. He didn't know what to do or think. The anger built inside of him. He quickly stood up and strode out of the room and down the stairs. Finding the butler, he started asking question after question about the person he let in. Jeremy must have been watching because he'd appeared in the same clothes as Anthony, which was why they let him in. He looked and was dressed the same.

They needed to call the constable, but he was sickened by everything. He went into the study and opened the liquor cabinet. Belting back the first one, he let the warmth seep through him. Now there were three more murders to add to the list.

~*~

Jeremy was out of the country before Anthony discovered the letter. He couldn't believe how well things were working out. He wished he could've seen Anthony's face when he realized that his parents were murdered. At the time, he didn't think Lexi surviving and telling everyone about him was a good thing, but now that he didn't have to hide he could torment Anthony more. The game had taken a turn and he was enjoying it.

– CHAPTER TEN –

E vie stood at the door to the study and watched Anthony staring down at the fire. The pain she felt for his loss was almost unbearable. If something like that had happened to her she knew how it would affect her. It had been a few, long hours while the police talked to everyone about Jeremy being there and the letter he'd left.

"Don't just stand there, come on in." He didn't turn to look away from the fire when she entered the room.

"I wasn't sure if you wanted to be alone."

"I've been alone for so long it seems. Would you like a drink?"

"Sure." Maybe getting drunk would be a good idea. Maybe they could forget about everything for a little bit.

Watching him walk to the bar to pour her a drink, she could tell by the tension in his body he was wound tight and seriously pissed off. He poured them both a drink, tipped his glass to her and they knocked it back.

Slamming the glass back onto the bar, Evie enjoyed the warmth seeping through her from the inside out.

"Come, let's sit by the fire." He grabbed the bottle and their glasses. He was quiet for a while as they stared into the flames.

"You know, I really had great parents. They were always there for me. Always encouraging me to try new things. I traveled the world with them as I was growing up. Later I traveled it on my own, but I always knew where home was; where *they* were."

"How was it growing up in different countries?"

He shrugged. "It's all I knew. I thought it was pretty great. The younger I was, the more I was confused by the different cultures. I was always getting things confused, or trying to explain to the other children what I was talking about."

"So you spent most of your time in the U. S. and UK right?"

"During the school years, yes. But when I was on holiday, we were all over the place. That is how I was able to learn so many languages."

The thought of him talking to her in a language she knew nothing about was a turn on. "How many do you know?"

"Five fluently, a couple of others enough to get by."

"Wow. That is so cool."

He chuckled at her. "Yes, it's the norm outside of the States to know more than one language."

"My upbringing was a little different. My parents loved to travel, but without children along. They made sure that they stayed near my grandparents so that Jackson and I had someone to watch us. That's where Jackson gets his wanderlust from. He's never been able to stay in one place for too long before moving on again."

"It must have been lonely for you. Did your parents love you at all?"

"Yes, they did, I didn't mean to give you that impression. They did, they just liked to travel more. When they were home it was all about us, but then they'd have to leave again. Lucky for me my grandparents were great. And the summers when Lexi was there were magical. We caused so much trouble." She laughed and told Anthony some of their adventures. They had a good laugh over how Lexi and Evie had locked Jackson out of the house while he was naked when he was a teenager during the middle of the day.

They sat in silence for a few minutes before Anthony turned to her and said, "I don't understand. Why are you doing this? Why put yourself in danger? Why subject yourself to seeing things you can never erase from your memory?"

Evie thought for a moment before replying. "Lexi has always been there for me. supported me. She followed me when I led us into trouble when we were younger. She always stuck up for me. No matter what. She was different after her first attack, anyone would be. But finally, finally she was getting back to her old self, and then she met Noah. You wouldn't believe the change in her. I got my Lexi back; I could hear it in her voice when we'd talk on the phone." She took another drink. "Then the second attack." She shook her head. "I really don't remember much of the drive to the hospital. I know I shouldn't have been on the road. But to see her like that again, I couldn't take it. She is so lucky to have Noah; they are really good for each other. She healed again. I really can't believe how strong she is."

"Then she got married. Everything was perfect. Except for all the extra security." She laughed without humor. "Noah went a bit overboard, but really I can't blame him. Their whole wedding day, which should've been a wonderful memory, there was a black cloud hanging over them. When we were getting ready, I'd see that look in Lexi's eyes and know she was thinking about Jeremy. Then I'd see Noah and he'd be scanning the crowd making sure he wasn't there. I can't see them living their whole life that way. That's why I e-mailed you. I was hoping we'd be able to work together to do something, anything, to catch Jeremy. It's my wedding gift to them. She's like my sister." She shrugged. "And now there's you."

Anthony sat up straight in his chair. "What do you mean there's me?"

The alcohol was making her bolder than usual. "Well, since we first heard about what Jeremy did I couldn't get you out of my head. What you went through, everything you'd lost. If there was a way I could help both of you, it was just something I had to do. That's how it started anyway. Then we started working together…"

They stared at each other, each trying to decide how much to say, or even what to say. Finally Evie spoke. "I can't deny the pull I feel when I'm around you."

She saw his eyes burn with passion before he closed them. When he opened them again after a moment the passion was gone. She felt he wasn't feeling the same things as her and it made her sad.

After the internal battle, he finally said, "Tell me why you decided to open a bookstore."

She let out the breath she'd been holding, not sure if she was relieved or sad they weren't going to be getting into a serious conversation about their feelings. She went on to tell him how she had always loved to read and loved nothing better than recommending a book to someone who ended up loving it.

She'd lost track of how many drinks they'd had while talking about the differences in their upbringing and Lexi. She giggled as she came back into the room. All the drinking was making her have to use the bathroom frequently. He still seemed like he was sober, especially compared to her. As she got closer to their chairs, she tripped over the rug and landed on his lap.

"Sorry." she laughed. "But I couldn't have done so well if I wasn't drinking." She tried to get up but his arms closed around her and held her there. Turning to look at him with a puzzled look in her eyes hoping him keeping her here was because he wanted her.

"Stay. Right here. Stay. I've been caged for so long. You've brought me back to life, given me a reason to do more than just put one foot in front of the other. I need you." With their eyes locked, he leaned in to gently kiss her.

Wrapping her arms around him, she let herself go and fall into the kiss. She couldn't keep her hands off of him and started running them over his hard muscles, she felt the heat build within her. Wanting more, she straddled him. When his hands moved under her shirt, she moaned into his mouth. Her head tipped back when he lifted it up moving her bra with the shirt out of the way, his mouth capturing her nipple. She started grinding on him, wanting more. She tried to get his shirt off. Since that wasn't working, she settled for taking her shirt and bra off giving him unlimited access.

He picked her up and moved closer to the fire and laid her down on the rug. She whimpered when he moved away but it was just to take his shirt off. He lay back down on top of her, the feel of skin on skin overwhelming. Looking at the shadows of his muscles in the firelight, she felt the fire burn in her. Grabbing him by the hair, she pulled him back to her mouth. Wanting dominance, she rolled them over so she was on top. It felt as if hands and lips were everywhere. When she felt his fingers along the waistband to her pants, she wanted to scream.

He tortured her by slowly removing the rest of her clothing, kissing all the way down then back up again. When he reached where she was dripping wet, his tongue and fingers flew at such a pace she went over the edge quickly. Looking at him through half closed eyes, she wanted more. She wanted to feel him inside her. When he took his pants off, she told herself to calm down and not tackle him. Once the condom was on, he moved like a predator towards her positioning himself between her legs.

Looking deep into her eyes, not yet inside, he paused. "Stop me now. Once isn't going to be enough. I'm going to want you forever. If you don't want that, stop me now."

There was nothing else she wanted more than him. "There is nothing that could make me stop you."

Feeling him slowly slide into her and fill her up, her eyes rolled back in her head and he captured her lips with his. Their pace picked up until the frenzy of their love-making shocked her. She loved the fact that he was so strong, he could move her from one position to another with little effort. When they both finally came, she was shocked at the intensity of it. Laying there shaking in his arms, she'd never felt so complete.

~*~

The last thing Evie remembered was Anthony carrying her up from the study to his room and putting her into bed. As his arms came around her, she fell into a dreamless sleep. Waking up and not feeling those arms around her made her heart fall. She feared he was having second thoughts. Rolling over she saw him sitting, fully clothed, in a chair by the window looking at her. They stared at each other for a few moments before he finally spoke.

"Our plane leaves in four hours, we'd better get moving."

"Well, good morning to you too." She threw the covers off and got out of bed. Naked, she stalked out of his room and went into hers. Throwing clothes into her suitcase, she called him every name she could think of.

"Very colorful language."

"What can I say? You bring out the best in me."

"Evie, last night…"

"Don't say it. Don't you dare say it." She whirled towards him and poked her finger in his chest.

"A mistake."

"No, it wasn't, there were two of us there. That isn't something that happens every day." She felt like her whole world tilted and she was no longer sure of anything.

"No, it's not. But think about it."

"Obviously, you have."

"Yes, I spent all night thinking about it. Being with you was the best night of my life but it can't happen again."

"Oh, now that makes perfect sense." She turned back around and started throwing the rest of her stuff in the suitcase with shaking hands trying not to scream.

Coming up behind her he grabbed her arm and turned her around, anger burning in his eyes. "Yes, it does. Think about it for a minute. Jeremy kills women that I am connected to. Now I've added you to the list. Do you think I want to see you end up like the others?" He gave her a little shake. "It would kill me if something happened to you. I can't risk that."

"So you'll just throw all of this away?" She gestured with her arms.

"If I have to. And God willing, it's not forever. Just until we catch him. I want you back at your grandmother's with extra security. I won't risk you. I can't lose you. Don't you understand?"

"I do, but you are completely wrong. You *need* me. Not just for this." She pointed to the two of them. "But for the investigation. I can help. Don't you dare push me away."

"You aren't going to back down are you?"

"Hell no. Are you?"

"Hell no."

"Fine, we'll just have to see who wins." She smacked him on the ass and walked into the bathroom to finish getting ready, making plans to break him first.

~*~

The trip through security at both airports was not as bad as it could have been. Anthony had set up with the local authorities to escort them to the airport with documentation that it was him and not Jeremy flying back to the States. There were more people waiting for them in Boston to make sure it was still him.

Their faces might look the same but at least their fingerprints were different. It was going to make traveling difficult, but they were willing to do whatever was needed to prove Anthony wasn't Jeremy so they could find the answers they needed.

– CHAPTER ELEVEN –

Evie moaned and rolled over, pulling the pillow over her head, wanting the person invading her sleep to go away.

"No way Sweet Cheeks, time to rise and shine!"

"Grandmother, *go away*." She didn't want to think of the fact she'd called Anthony Sweet Cheeks.

"Nope, you've got to get up."

Glaring at her smiling grandmother she said, "It had better be worth it."

"Oh, it is. Totally. Now come downstairs for something to eat. You've slept long enough."

"I'll be the judge of that."

"No sass. Now move it!" Evelyne laughed as she left the room ducking the pillow Evie threw at her head.

"Fine." She tossed the covers off and tried to make herself presentable. She saw her open suitcase still sitting there waiting to be unpacked. She walked over to it and bent down picking up the shirt she was wearing when she and Anthony made love. Bringing it up to her face, she could smell his scent on it. Closing her eyes, she wanted to remember that scent forever.

~*~

Evelyne wouldn't tell Evie what was going on until she ate something and filled her in about what had happened overseas. Her grandmother was very upset about adding three more murders to Jeremy's growing list.

"I think you should stay away from Anthony."

"Why?"

"Why? Gee, I don't know. Maybe because I don't want to see you added to the list."

"Anthony says the same thing."

"Oh, he does. Well, that's good."

"You weren't expecting that. Ha! That is awesome."

"Shut up. Can you please stay away from him?"

"No, which is what I've already told him. When have you ever known me to back down?"

"Never. Damn it."

Evie leaned over and kissed her grandmother on the cheek. "You should know better. I'm too much like you."

"Stop. Are you ready for the big news?"

Pushing her plate away Evie bounced in her chair. "Yes, tell me!"

"Lexi and Noah are back."

Evie was torn. She sat there quietly looking at the crumbs on the table.

"I thought you'd be more excited."

"I am. Just wondering what I'm going to say to her about Anthony."

"Yeah, you should worry about that."

"Not helping."

At the sound of the doorbell, her grandmother jumped up. "Too late. There she is. Jackson is taking me to meet the ladies. That will give you some time to talk to Lexi without everyone around."

"Thanks, Grandma." Evie walked to the door and opened it to her best friend. Marriage agreed with her and with a squeal they hugged each other tight. "Looking good, you old, married woman."

"Hahaha! Evelyne have anything sweet to eat? I'm starving."

"You know she always does." Evie turned to the quiet woman who came in behind Lexi. "Kat, would you like anything?"

"No, thank you. I'm fine." Kat said as she stood at the back of the room.

"Have a seat, I'll be right back." Evie walked out of the room and got them something sweet to eat and to drink.

"Tell me all about your honeymoon. Well, not all of it. I'm not as bad as the Troublesome Trio."

Lexi laughed. "It was so wonderful. I can't believe Noah rented out a whole island for us. It was so wonderful even if the place was crawling with security. And we were able to get some sightseeing in."

"Was that all you did all day?"

"Nope, but that's all I'm going to tell you about." Lexi winked at her and proceeded to tell her all the places they had gone and seen and the people they'd met.

Evie sat up. "Hey, wait a minute. I thought you were going to be back next week at the earliest."

Lexi smiled at her. "We were, but then…"

"But then what? Tell me, damn it."

"Well, it seems someone doesn't trust foreign doctors. Even ones that are world-renowned."

"Doctors? Are you okay? What's wrong?" Evie moved closer shaking Lexi's arm.

She frowned as Lexi laughed at her. "I'm fine. In fact, I've never been better. And in just over eight months we'll be…"

Evie screamed and started jumping up and down shouting, "You're pregnant! Oh my god, you're fucking pregnant! Oops." She sat back down and patted Lexi's stomach, "Sorry little one, I'll try to be better with my language."

"I don't think the little one can understand you yet." She patted her stomach.

"Ha-ha. Oh my gosh! I'm so excited. How's Noah? I bet he's over the moon. Tell me everything."

"I will, if you'll give me a chance."

"Sorry."

"He's crazy happy. I've had to try to stop him from buying every baby item out there. I figure we should, at least, wait until we know if we are having a boy or a girl."

"Well, yeah. Totally makes sense. We're going to have to get together and celebrate. Well, some of us anyway."

"I can still have a glass of wine a week."

"We will plan around that then." Pulling her into a tight hug. "I'm so happy for you. I can't wait to see the proud papa. We should start planning."

"Planning? Really Evie, it's a bit…"

"Evie, can I talk to you…"

Lexi jumped up off of the couch and screamed at the sight of Anthony standing there.

In slow motion, Evie saw Kat pull the gun out of her holster and point it at Anthony.

"No!" Evie screamed as she jumped in front of Anthony. "It's not Jeremy. Kat please put the gun down."

"Never," she hissed. "Move out of the way."

"Stop. Please. Really it's Anthony. He's come here to get answers about Jeremy." She was fighting against Anthony as he tried to push her out of the way.

"Evie move, I don't want her to shoot you." Anthony pleaded.

"How can you be sure it's not Jeremy?" asked Kat.

Not taking her eyes off of Kat, Evie reached around to pull Anthony's arm in front of her. "See? No scar."

Evie let out a breath as Kat lowered her weapon even though she didn't holster it. She finally looked over at Lexi who was backed into the corner of the room with her hand over her mouth. "I'm sorry Lexi. I was going to tell you. I just hadn't gotten a chance yet."

Lowering her hand and sidestepping towards Kat, Lexi glared at her. "Yeah, is there really ever a good time to bring up the fact that you've got someone who looks just like the bastard that left me to die twice living with you? Come on Kat, let's go."

"Please Lexi, let me explain."

"Save it." The door slammed as they left.

Anthony's arms came around her holding her tight against him. "I'm so sorry, la mia belezza. I didn't know she was here."

Leaning her head back against his chest she said, "I know. I've got to go explain things to her."

"I'm not sure now is the best time."

"It never will be. It will be better going to her place, Noah will be there. Plus all the other security. She'll feel safe."

"I hope you're right. Please make sure she knows it was never my intention to scare her."

Running her hands up and down the arms that were wrapped around her waist she said, "I know. I'll be back soon."

~*~

118

Evie was distraught while driving to Noah's. She was shaking by the time she got there and went through security to get to his home. For a moment, she worried that Lexi would tell them not to let her in.

Noah opened the door for her and pulled her in for a hug. Evie relaxed into him for a moment.

"You've really pissed her off."

"I know, I'm so sorry. I didn't have a chance to tell her what was going on."

"Well, here's your chance. We're in the kitchen. Come on. The best way is to just get it over with."

"And you know this how?"

"I married the woman and love pushing her buttons. It's become a hobby for me. I'm interested to hear what you have to say, too."

Evie almost broke down into tears seeing Lexi sitting there looking so lost. She went over and knelt down in front of her taking her hands in hers. "I'm so sorry. Please let me explain."

"You've got five minutes." Lexi wouldn't meet her eyes.

"Anthony rented Grandma's cottage. We didn't know that until he showed up one day. After a short time of him proving he wasn't Jeremy and explaining why he's here, I decided to help him. Don't you understand, Lexi? He wants Jeremy found even more than you do! You don't know what that bastard has taken from him. We just found out he killed Anthony's parents. His list of victims keeps growing with every new piece of the puzzle we find. Please understand, you know I can help."

Lexi sat there for a few moments lost in thought. "It was just a shock to see him standing there. Right now, I can't separate the two in my mind. Why did he come here?"

"He wants to talk to you." Hearing Lexi's gasp, Evie continued on. "He's hoping that you will remember something, anything that might help us. We've already talked to people in the area where he stayed and the ex-husband of the lady that was murdered here. It gave us another name, Jay Ellison. We found property in New York and went there."

"Did you find anything else?"

"He knows Anthony is searching for him. He's left letters for him at both the New York home and Anthony's home in London. He's one sick bastard and he's got to be caught. You could help with that."

Lexi got up and started pacing the room. "How can I help him? It makes me sick just to look at him."

"Lexi, they are two different people," Noah said quietly from the other side of the room.

Lexi whirled on him. "Don't you think I know that? Don't you think it makes me sick that I put him away for years for doing nothing? Nothing Noah, absolutely nothing!" She sat down hard. "I still hate myself for that."

Evie got up and walked towards her. "I know, honey, but this is your chance to help out. There might be some little thing that wouldn't mean anything to anyone else but Anthony. Some little thing that might help us catch him before he kills again. Because he will, it's just a matter of time."

Noah came over and sat down next to Lexi putting his arm around her. "She's right, you know. As much as you hate all of this, not helping when you have the chance will eat at you. You can set the terms. We can meet here, anything to make you as comfortable as can be."

Leaning her head on Noah's shoulder Lexi said, "I don't know when I'll be ready."

"It's got to be sooner, rather than later. Jeremy has to know with Anthony knowing about his parents, he's going to be coming harder and faster to find him and make him pay."

The two friends stared at each other. Lexi took a deep breath. "Tomorrow. Both of you come here tomorrow. We'll go over everything."

Evie hugged her. "Thank you. I love you."

"I love you, too, now go. I think I need to lie down."

Evie and Noah watched her walk out of the room. "Please make sure she gets some rest tonight."

"I'll do my best. But you know Lexi…"

"Yes, I do. Oh, and make sure you have everything you've got on Jeremy handy. He stole all of our paperwork in London. We've got a lot to go over."

"Sure, I'll see if I can get any other information on Jay Ellison while I'm at it."

"Thanks, and Noah, keep her safe, that sicko is still out there."

"That's my mission. See you tomorrow."

The sun was setting as Evie drove home. Distracted, she didn't notice the headlights following her.

– CHAPTER TWELVE –

Evie walked slowly up to the cottage door. Before she could knock, the door flung open and she was pulled into a hug. Laying her head on his chest, she breathed in the scent she could recognize anywhere.

"Come in, I was worried about you. I hated the fact that I couldn't go with you. It's been the longest two hours of my life."

"I was just at Lexi and Noah's. There was security all over the place."

"I know, but I was worried about the drive to and from there. Anything could have happened. Now that you are here I thought I'd cook you dinner."

"You can cook?"

He messed up her hair. "Yes, I can cook. Nothing fancy, my mom made sure I knew how to cook. She said it would keep me from starving or dying early from eating fast food all the time."

"Well, whip me something up, Chef Maldono."

Grinning over his shoulder at her he said, "You kinky thing you."

"Ha-ha." She sat down on the couch and watched him work in the kitchen while she filled him in at how things went with Lexi and Noah. There was something sexy about a man comfortable in the kitchen.

"Noah sounds like a sensible man."

"He has his moments. He's really good for Lexi. He's totally there for her, to back her up or make her see things another way. Then there are the times he can be a goofball and keeps her off-guard, which she needs."

"She has changed so much since the last time I saw her."

It was strange to think Lexi and Anthony had once dated. That the last time they had seen each other was in a courtroom.

"There is something else you need to know before we go over there tomorrow."

He turned to her. "What?"

"Lexi's pregnant. That means Noah is going to do whatever it takes to keep her safe."

Anthony bowed his head. "I'd do the same." Looking at Evie, she could see the anguish in his eyes. "He's got to be caught, and soon. For all we know, he's given up on Lexi, but we can't take that chance. He might have a new obsession." He stared at Evie. She shivered at the intense look in his eyes, knowing his protective instincts were for her.

~*~

After dinner, Evie was doing the dishes while Anthony dug around the board games for something to play. They'd decided they needed a break from all the doom and gloom. They couldn't stay away from each other. She was happy when he kept coming up with ideas to keep her close by.

The window above the sink was open and the cool night air was coming through it. Lost in thought, she didn't hear anyone approach. She stood there frozen in horror as a face popped up on the other side of the screen. The face that was so much like Anthony's.

"You're even prettier close up," he whispered and proceeded to lick the screen leaving drops of saliva behind. "I can't wait to see how you bleed." With a manic laugh, he disappeared.

Evie screamed for Anthony who came running. She had barely gotten the words out when he grabbed a baseball bat and ran out of the cottage telling her to stay put.

Quickly she ran over to the door and locked it. With her gut in turmoil and shaking hands, she proceeded to close every window and close the drapes. She was afraid he was going to pop up again. In the kitchen, she grabbed the biggest knife she could find and armed herself with it.

Frantically, looking around the small cottage. She didn't know where to hide. She went into the bathroom and locked the door, but scenes of *Psycho* and *The*

Shining ran through her head. She didn't want to be trapped in here with no way out. Settling on standing against the only wall in the cottage that didn't have a window, she kept looking around waiting for him to burst through a window.

"Shit," she said. There on the kitchen counter was her phone. She should have already called the police. Making a dash for it she grabbed it and returned to her spot. It took her three tries to finally be able to press the numbers 911.

Feeling better that the police were on the way she sat and waited, watching the clock. Hearing a key in the lock her heart leaped into her throat. For a moment she was happy to see Anthony, she started towards him and stopped. *What if it's not him?*

Holding the knife in front of her she said, "Stop right there. How do I know who you are?"

"Evie it's me, Anthony."

It sounded like Anthony but she couldn't be sure. "How do I know he didn't find you and bash you over the head, steal your clothes and come back here?"

Anthony rolled up his sleeves to show her it was him. Dropping her weapon she rushed and jumped into his arms. "Oh thank God, I was so scared."

"Everything's ok. The bastard is quick. He had a car waiting. I couldn't get the plate number."

"Shit." She pulled back from him and hit him in the chest. "What the hell were you doing going out there by yourself? He could have killed you!"

"No, he wouldn't. Think about it, I wouldn't suffer near enough."

There was a knock on the door, Evie took that opportunity to call Noah and let him know that Jeremy was in the area. She also called Jackson so that he could make sure their grandmother was safe.

After the police left, Anthony leaned up against the door tilting his head back and closing his eyes. Evie could feel the exhaustion coming off him in waves. She went and wrapped her arms around him. They stayed that way for a while before either one of them said what was on their minds.

"I don't know what to do. Should I leave? Will that keep you safe? Or should I stay and hope I can protect you? Hearing what he said to you makes me want to rip him apart with my bare hands."

Evie shivered. She didn't want to think about those words. "I don't think leaving is the right option. We pick the place, not him. Besides, maybe we could use me as bait."

He pushed her aside and started pacing. "Are you completely and utterly out of your mind? You've got to be kidding me. You know what he is capable of. What if the plan doesn't work? I will not have you as another victim. I couldn't live with myself if something happened to you. I won't have that on my conscience."

She walked up to him and laid her hands on his face bringing it close to hers. "Exactly. I trust you.

We'll come up with something and we'll make sure we think of everything. We've got to end this."

"We'll talk about this later. Right now, we both need some sleep. Tomorrow is going to be a rough day."

"Yes, it will be. But hopefully something will come of it. But I'm not sure how I will be able to sleep knowing he is here."

"Do you want to go out to Noah's? At least, that way you will be surrounded by security."

"What and leave you here by yourself? Not a chance."

"I'm a big boy. I can take care of myself."

"Yes, you can, but that doesn't mean I still won't worry. Nope, I'm staying here."

"Fine, I'll walk you home."

"No, here as in the cottage."

"Like hell."

"Like hell, I am."

"No."

"Yes. You know I can do this all night. You might as well give in. If it makes you feel any better, I'll sleep on the couch. That way you won't have to worry about your virtue." She was willing to do whatever it took in order to be close to him. It always made her feel better, safer to be near him.

"Come here." He held his hand out to her. She walked over, placing hers in his, and he pulled her close. "I would feel better knowing exactly where you are. But we'll have to sleep in the same bed. I don't want you in the other room."

Evie hoped they would both be able to get some sleep. But if they were going to stay awake, might as well make it torture on him.

"I need to get some things at the house for the night."

"Let's go."

~*~

Jeremy sat there and stared at the screen, there was Evie washing the dishes. He was happy that he had thought ahead to wear a camera for tonight's adventures. Watching as her face filled the screen as he approached the window, the horror on her face was priceless. He froze the picture when her mouth was open. Stroking himself harder and harder until he finally came, spewing cum all over her face on the screen.

– CHAPTER THIRTEEN –

Evie walked into her grandmother's house in a bad mood. It did not get any better seeing Jackson there waiting for her.

"'Bout time you showed up. Doing the walk of shame?"

"Perv. No, there is no walk of shame." *Not for lack of trying on my part.*

He stopped her when she tried to walk by. "Do you really think this is the smartest thing to do?"

"What are you talking about Oh Wise One?"

"Spending all this time with Anthony? Spending the night over there? Come on, he's got a psychopath stalker killing people he's close to and you can't get closer than sleeping together."

"That is all we did. Sleep."

"Ahh... so that's what has you in such a pissy mood. No nookie for you."

"Shut up. We are going to Lexi and Noah's in a bit to go over everything."

"Really? This I've got to see. I'm coming."

"No, you're not."

"It's not up to you. I'll call Lexi, I'm sure she'd love me to be there. Or maybe Noah, we seemed to hit it off."

"No, Jackson, you can't go. Who's going to keep an eye on Grandma?" She thought she had him there.

"Not a problem, I'll drop her off with the rest of the Trio, remember, it's Thursday."

"Fuck."

He just laughed at her.

A thought crossed her mind. "You know, someone really needs to stay with them and make sure they don't get into any trouble."

"Not going to work. They've been going without supervision for years. They can't get into much trouble."

"Famous last words."

"Plus Noah, put a security detail on them after last night."

"Oh, they will love that."

"Yeah, Grams is up there putting on her makeup right now."

"Wonderful."

"Now, you need to move it. I'm ready, but seriously, Sis, you need some work. You look like shit."

"Asshole." She punched him in the stomach as she walked by, satisfied when he grunted in pain.

~*~

"Shotgun," Jackson yelled as he raced to the car.

"Grow up." Evie yelled after him.

"Never!" He tried to open the door and frowned when it was locked.

Anthony held up the keyfob to him. "Ladies should always get their choice of seats."

Jackson scowled at him. "Have you met my sister? I don't think 'lady' is even in her vocabulary."

Anthony raised his eyebrows at him. "And a true gentlemen would never even dream of saying something like that about any woman."

Evie walked over and thrust her hip toward Jackson's to bump him out of the way nodding towards Anthony. "See? You could learn a lot from him." She just grinned as Anthony opened the door and helped her in.

She couldn't hear what they said to each other after her door was closed but based on the grim looks on their faces, it wasn't good. She looked back over her shoulder and gave her brother a look, she never liked it when he went all protective big brother on her.

~*~

Evie was so happy when they finally pulled into Lexi and Noah's. She wanted to slap Jackson so bad. He had scooted up so that his head was in between theirs, talking the whole time about growing up and how much trouble Evie got into.

Noah stood at the door waiting for them. Before anyone could say anything, he spoke. "I'll kick you out of here so fast you won't know what hit you if this gets too much for Lexi."

Anthony nodded. "I understand. I'd feel the same way. Thank you for allowing this."

Evie snorted. "Oh, and like Lexi has no say in the matter. Men."

Noah grabbed her in a headlock. "You know what we meant."

"Yes, us poor, little, weak women. We couldn't make a decision on our own if it wasn't for you big, strong men." She batted her eyes at him. After elbowing him in the gut so that he'd let her go, she said, "Now where are the womenfolk? I need more estrogen."

Evie walked into the room and saw Lexi standing by the kitchen counter with Kat right next to her. She thought she heard her brother gasp but when she turned around he had his poker face on.

Not sure on what to do next, Evie walked over to Lexi giving her a hug. "Thank you," she whispered in her ear.

Taking a deep breath, Lexi stepped forward. With tears in her eyes she said to Anthony, "I'm so sorry. I didn't know. I can't image what you have gone through, and part of it is my fault."

Anthony stayed where he was. "It's really not your fault. I just hope one day you can see the man I am and not him."

"Well, she's not going to have to worry about that since you'll be leaving soon and she'll never see you again," Kat said from the background.

Evie turned to Kat. "What makes you say that?"

"He's got no reason to be here. He gets what he wants and leaves. Isn't that what you do?"

Evie was surprised by the venom in Kat's words. They'd spent time together since she was always by Lexi's side, but she knew her to be reserved and not say much. Every once in a while, she would let loose and they were able to have some laughs.

"Kat!" Evie could tell by the sound of Lexi's voice that she was just as shocked by what Kat had said.

Kat looked down. "Sorry. It's just that for over a year now all I have done is studied everything about Anthony and Jeremy; looking at picture after picture, knowing what he is capable of. Watching over Lexi so that Jeremy doesn't get another chance. So to see him," she pointed to Anthony, "being able to just walk right in here. It makes my trigger finger twitch."

Noah walked over to Lexi and moved her away from Kat. "Well, maybe you should leave. We can have someone else come up here while Anthony is here."

She shook her head. "No, *I* can control myself."

Evie wondered what she was really getting at. She moved over to Anthony and grabbed his hand so that he was forced to follow her to the living room. She felt a tingle between her shoulder blades but she was sure it was worse for Anthony. After sitting down, so they were facing everyone else she said, "Let's get started."

~*~

They worked long into the evening. Sam and Martha made sure that they had enough food and were taken care of. Between Noah's and Anthony's men they had a lot of paperwork.

Evie's anxiety increased as the sun went down. Knowing Jeremy was close by and the curtains were open wasn't helping. She finally had to say something and Noah pushed a button and all of the curtains came down. Feeling like she could concentrate again, they got back to it.

They created a map of the murders and a summary of each. Going over what Anthony and Evie had learned about Natalie Sutton, Anthony's parents, and Christina Cooper.

"So Lexi, based on what Jeremy told you Tiffani was the first right?" asked Jackson.

"Yes. From what he said he loved her but she dumped him for Anthony. He couldn't take that and killed her. He tried to set Anthony up, but he was out with a friend that night."

"An old friend popped into town that day and called me last minute to go have a drink. He just went through a bad break-up and wanted some advice. Lucky for me, I guess."

"Then there was Natalie, the maid, and Anthony's parents. Boy, he was busy there for a few months.

Between that and the model in Paris, Monique Diaz that makes his murders international. Not too smart there." Evie was letting Jackson go through all of this. He was late to the game and she knew that talking it out was how he processed.

"We didn't get a chance to go over to Paris while we were in London. After finding out my parents were murdered, I wanted to get back here as soon as possible. Besides, a friend had set us up to go to that art opening together. We'd never met before then, another spur of the moment thing." Anthony shrugged.

"As far as the police reports go, they found nothing unusual about her or what led up to her murder."

"Next," Jackson continued, "We have the first grade teacher that was at a conference in L.A., Chelle Michaels. Yet again, another where circumstances came together and she was murdered. So far, five had some kind of long term relationship with Anthony; the next two were essentially in the wrong place at the wrong time."

"Then there was Heather Roberts. Now she was a kick-boxing instructor, so you would assume she had some moves on her. That must mean she was completely taken by surprise. Although, all Jeremy had to do was show up as you." He nodded towards Anthony. "And he'd be in. She would've let her guard down. But they never found her. That makes me wonder. Did he really kill her, or maybe she just took off on her own to start a new life."

Evie thought about that for a minute. "It would make sense except for the fact she was part owner in the boxing club. She would've drained her portion of the business down. She had two children and by all accounts they were a close, loving family. No, I don't think she just took off. We need to find some way to put Jeremy at each of the locations."

"Airline manifests? Is that even possible?" asked Jackson.

Anthony thought for a moment. "I might be able to get them. Not sure if it is completely legal, but I know someone who might be able to."

Evie jumped up. "If we can see flights around the same time the murders took place, we might be able to tie it to him."

"It will take a couple of days, at least," Anthony said.

"Well, then why don't we take a trip to St. Thomas? Since she was never found it seems like a good place to start." Evie said.

"Why do you have to go?" Lexi asked quietly.

Evie walked over and sat down next to her. "Because I have to. Because I can. This is what I can do to help."

"I don't like it."

"Neither do I. If I had it my way, she wouldn't be going at all. But the stubborn woman she is, she'd probably just hop a flight and follow me," Anthony stated.

Lexi gave a little laugh. "You *do* know her well." She looked between the two of them.

Clearing his throat, Jackson continued. "So then we have Lexi. And Anthony going to prison. As far as we can tell, he didn't kill again until Christina Cooper. Which brings us back to Lexi again. Is that it?"

Evie and Anthony looked at each other before Anthony said, "Not quite. When we were searching his New York apartment, we found another woman. The police have tried to keep it quiet but the lady's name was Jackie Olsen. She had been seeing someone for the past year, but none of her friends had ever seen him. They searched her place and found DNA that matches Jeremy. It appears that he's becoming sloppy since he has nothing to hide now."

"That poor woman. To be fooled for so long and to have it end that way." Lexi said.

"Just be thankful you didn't see it." Evie shuddered.

"He's got to be stopped." Noah's fist hit the table.

"That he does. So Anthony and I will take a quick trip. Hopefully the information we need will be here when we get back. Then we can all start going through it and see where it takes us."

Lexi got up and hugged Evie tight. "Please stay safe. After everything he's taken I couldn't bear it if I lost you, too. I love you."

"I love you, too." Evie looked at Anthony over Lexi's head. Her attention was sidetracked by the look of hatred on Kat's face. It would seem Kat was having a hard time separating the two men.

~*~

Jeremy rubbed his hands together. It couldn't be going any better if he'd planned the whole thing himself. Thinking it was a stroke of genius, he'd made up for Lexi and Noah a plaque from the Humane Society thanking them for their donation that said 'Pepper's Grub – Keep your paws off.' As he was hoping, they put it above her food and water dishes, which gave him the perfect view of the living room from the kitchen. Since he had made sure someone from the Humane Society had delivered it to them somehow, thankfully it had bypassed security. He was able to see and hear everything that was said. Laughing at the fact it hadn't been discovered yet, he listened closely to what was being said just a few miles from where he was.

– CHAPTER FOURTEEN –

Anthony and Evie were able to get a flight out the next morning so by late afternoon they were in the warm tropics. Since there was nothing they could do until tomorrow, they decided to have a nice dinner on the patio of their room. Anthony didn't want them in separate rooms, not even adjoining and Evie had to admit, she was happy they would be sharing a bed.

Her hopes were dashed when he fell asleep quickly. Lying there staring at the ceiling, she wondered how one moment he could be so protective and loving and the next turn it off. She supposed it had to do with all of the loss he's suffered and being locked up for all those years.

Turning over, she memorized his face, softened in sleep, the lines between his eyebrows gone. She knew she was falling for him and besides not being what she wanted in this stage of her life, it would affect Lexi. They would see each other all the time, that constant reminder. All Evie could hope for was time healing their wounds and getting Jeremy locked up so they wouldn't have to worry about that any more.

Tentatively, she reached out and ran a finger down the side of his face. When he didn't move, she became braver. Moving down towards his lips, remembering them on her, wanting them there again.

Suddenly, her hand was grabbed and she was pinned beneath him. His eyes glowed with anger in the moonlight coming through the window. Seeing the recognition come into them his body relaxed but he did not move from on top of her.

"I'm sorry." She was slightly scared by the look in his eyes, but knew he wouldn't do anything to hurt her.

Dipping his head so that their foreheads touched, he said, "No, I'm sorry. I didn't mean to scare you."

She waited for him to open his eyes and look into hers. When he did, something changed between them. He slowly tilted his head and gently captured her lips with his.

Hands gently stroked each other, the kiss deepened. Evie wasn't wearing much in an attempt to torment him so it made easy access for him to reach down between her legs. He moaned when he found she was only wearing a very small thong.

He moved down her body spending considerable about of time teasing her nipples with his mouth and fingers before he moved further down and buried his mouth in her wetness. She thought she'd come up off of the bed with the pleasure his fingers and tongue gave her.

Feeling the orgasm build, she wanted him inside of her so badly, "Please, I need you inside of me," she begged but he wasn't budging until she went over the edge. Finally, Evie screamed his name. Anthony moved quickly up the bed until he was buried deep inside of her. She still quaked from her release. As he thrust harder and faster, she felt another one build around him. Evie raked her nails down his back and neither one was able to hold on and they both tumbled over the edge together.

With his weight on top of her, she ran her fingers lightly across his skin. This is where she wanted to be. This felt like home. She wanted to stay this way forever. Too soon, he moved off of her. Before she could protest he pulled her into his arms and covered them.

"Sleep, la mia belezza."

She was unable to keep her eyes open. Drifting off to sleep quickly, they didn't notice the reflection of the camera from a nearby balcony.

~*~

There must have been something in the air because it felt like they were on vacation. They were both lighter and flirted with each other. Heading out to the marina, the morning sky was clear and blue. In their research they found out that a Jay Ellison had rented a boat from one of the businesses at the marina.

"Good Morning, and welcome to Eilina's Boat Rentals. I'm Kaitlin, how may I help you?"

"Hello, Kaitlin, my name is Anthony. I believe one of my associates spoke to you regarding a rental from a few years ago."

"Oh yes, they actually spoke with my husband Jake. I think he was getting the information together, hold on." She walked out of the room and returned a few minutes later with Jake.

"Howdy, come on back, I've got some stuff for you."

"Walking into the back room, Evie looked around and saw the walls covered with pictures of their family, including a little boy that was completely adorable. She focused on what Jake was telling Anthony.

"So Jay chartered a boat for the day, leaving at seven in the morning. I've got down that there were two people aboard. I saw him and a young lady board, but when he came back, it was only him that came back into the office. I remember, because I thought it was strange. He told me that she was really seasick and took her to the car before coming in."

"Did you happen to catch her name?" Evie asked.

"No, I didn't, didn't even think about it." Jake said.

"Any idea where they might have gone?" Anthony asked.

"I can do better than that. I can show you." He reached over and brought out a map and marked on it. "There is a little island out here, not too many people go out there. I've got all of the boats equipped with GPS and record where they go and how long they were there. It helps if a boat doesn't come back. And I hate to say it, but sometimes people rent boats for illegal purposes. I always keep it, no matter how long."

Evie and Anthony looked at each other with a sense of excitement and dread.

Anthony turned to Jake, "We're going to need to rent a boat."

~*~

After a quick trip back to the hotel and into town for supplies, they were back at the marina and on the boat preparing to set sail.

Watching Anthony at the wheel, his legs spread to keep his stance steady on the open sea, Evie was struck by his confidence steering the boat. They slowed as they neared the island.

Evie turned to him and said, "Well, at least we know why she stood you up. He met her early and she thought it was you."

Anthony shook his head, "I just don't understand how he can always find information out and stay one step ahead of me for so long now."

"Me either, but he can only do that for so long. I think we're catching up to him."

"I hope you're right. Based on the information Jake gave us, there is really only two places that you can get close to the island, this is one of them." He cut the motor. "But we still have to get out and swim through the water."

Looking at the island Evie shuddered. "Do we really have to search the whole thing?"

"I don't think we can. He said most of it is too rocky to get too far in without climbing gear. We've got to assume that with that short of notice he wouldn't do that. I've never been rock climbing, so it's not something he would have to learn."

"Good, let's do this." She took her clothes off so that she was in her white bikini. Catching him looking, she said, "Like what you see?"

"And then some." He proceeded slowly lift his shirt over his head before looking up at her and giving her a wink before unzipping his pants.

All Evie could do was stare. There are men that should never wear Speedos, and then there are men that should *only* wear Speedos. Anthony was one of those men. Evie didn't want to see him in anything else. She did have to hold back a chuckle at the fact that both of their suits were white.

Anthony dove into the water first and Evie licked her lips watching his form flow through the crystal clear water. When he came up, she handed him the waterproof bag that would hold their shoes. Thankful for her diving lessons when she was a teenager, she dove in after him. The water was warm as she moved gracefully through it.

They made a quick search of the small part of the island they could get to. Finding nothing, they went back to the boat. Watching him climb into the boat was a beautiful sight, the water dripping down his skin leaving trails of goose bumps as the breeze hit it.

They sat back and enjoyed a cool drink and snack. Looking around Evie wondered about the water. "Do you think he'd dump her in the water?"

Anthony thought about it. "Maybe. The water is really clear around here, I think it would be harder to disguise."

"But he'd only have to have it disguised for a bit before the natural underwater life would take it over."

"True, but it would be easier to dump her on the island."

"You'd think, but there is so little area that we could get to."

"Let's look on the other side of the island, and then if we can't find anything there, we can search the water around the island."

~*~

Finding nothing on the other side of the island, they searched the water. At this point, Anthony wasn't holding out much hope of finding anything. There were miles of ocean where a body could have been dumped.

It was slow work and neither of them knew what they were exactly looking for, so there were many dives down to find out it was nothing. Luckily, they'd brought snorkeling gear.

When they were almost back to where they had begun, Evie shouted, "Stop the boat."

Watching her shaking finger point to something under the water Anthony was filled with dread. He dropped anchor and hoped it was just the shadows playing tricks on them.

Turning to Evie, he knew he couldn't let her go down there. They had been taking turns and it was hers. "I'll go."

"No, it's my turn."

"Evie, please. Tell me, if it is what it looks like do you really want to go down there?"

Folding her arms across her chest, she said, "No, but you know I will."

He wrapped her in his arms. "Yes, I know you would, but please, just let me do this. If it is her, let me be the one to find her. I'm the reason she's down there."

"Fine."

Chuckling he said, "You're always so gracious."

"Go. We've been out here all day and it's going to be dark soon." She shivered.

"Yes, dear."

Sticking her tongue out, she handed him his gear. "Be careful."

"Always, la mia belezza."

Taking a deep breath, he dove into the water. All the sounds became muffled and it was just him and the fish in the water. As he grew closer, it became more and more clear that it was a skeleton. He didn't want to get too close, but he needed more information before going back up. Closing his eyes when he saw the mouth open in a silent scream, he hoped her death came quick. Swimming around, he saw there were chains around her, holding her under the water. He thought he saw a purse but he couldn't be sure and didn't want to disturb the evidence.

Swimming up to the surface, he wondered how Evie would take the news. This wasn't the first time they came across a dead body together. Jeremy needed to be stopped.

Pulling himself into the boat Evie must have sensed that it wasn't good news because she launched herself into his arms. Holding on tight, he closed his eyes in a silent prayer for the woman at the bottom of the ocean.

"Is it her?"

"I can't tell. There is a purse, so I'm assuming it's a woman. Hopefully the authorities will be able to tell."

"Shit."

"Exactly."

"What should we do now?"

"Head back into town and I expect spend a long night with the local police."

"Great. Well let's get this over with."

After they dressed, he started the boat and turned it around for the trip back to St. Thomas. Sensing her emotions were on overdrive, he held out his hand. Once it was in his he pulled her so she was in standing in front of him, resting her body on his. He could feel her shaking and wanted to take all this mess away from her.

Heading into the setting sun it would have been romantic, but the thought of a woman long dead at the bottom of the ocean couldn't leave him. They were almost back to the island when out of the corner of his eye he saw a boat speeding towards them.

Slightly changing his course so they wouldn't collide, he was shocked when the boat changed its course also.

"Hang on," he shouted to Evie. She dropped to the floor and moved out of his way. Barely glancing at her to make sure she was safe, he concentrated on the game of chicken this other boat was playing. His timing had to be perfect. At the last second, he jerked the wheel to the left hoping the other boat wouldn't do the same.

Quickly straightening the boat out, he pushed on full speed to the island. Looking back over his shoulder he saw the other boat turn around and start to chase them. The other boat was faster so Anthony had to be smarter. He wasn't sure who was driving it but he was afraid he knew. While he wanted nothing more than to destroy that monster, even at the sake of his own life, he wouldn't put Evie in that kind of danger.

He looked down and saw her watching him with huge eyes. "Get a life jacket and put it on."

"What about you?"

"I can't deal with it right now. Just take care of yourself."

Knowing that the fastest way between two points was a straight line, Anthony didn't deviate from the harbor. As the lights came closer, he was feeling optimistic. When he felt Evie come up by him, he checked to make sure she had the vest on and was going to yell at her to get back down when she managed to put a waist life preserver around his waist.

"I'll take care of you." She sat back down.

Turning around he saw the boat was too close for comfort. Taking a few extra seconds, he tried to get a look at the driver but it was getting too dark and it looked like they had something over their head.

"See if we've got cell phone service," he shouted to Evie. "We're close enough to shore now."

Hearing her shout to someone on the other end of the line made him breathe a little easier. Now if someone could get to them quickly, everything should be fine. His heart was beating so hard he could feel it throughout his whole body. He had to keep Evie safe and out of that monster's hands.

He kept searching the horizon for a boat to come racing from the harbor and turning around to see how close the other boat was. Now only feet separated them. Not sure what the other driver had in mind, Anthony thought about taking a chance and ramming the other boat. He was afraid with dark approaching they would have a hard time being found if the boat became too damaged to drive, or they were in the water.

The choice was taken out of his hands as the boat caught up to them and smashed into the side of their boat. It took all that Anthony had to hang on and not fall. He quickly looked down and saw Evie still hanging onto a pole with blood dripping down the side of her head.

Searching to see where the other boat was, his heart dropped as he saw it approaching them. With the motor starting to sputter he knew they didn't have much time left before they would be dead in the water. Judging the time, he cut the engine at the precise moment so that the other boat passed by them without hitting them.

He tried to start the boat up, but it wouldn't. "Shit. Come on. Come on. Start."

"Anthony?"

"Stand up. You might have to jump overboard."

The smell of gasoline filled the area. A gas line must have broken. He kept trying just in case. He could hear the roar of the other motor as it came closer. Turning to Evie he grabbed her hand. "We're going to have to jump and try to stay together."

Seeing her nod, they were prepared to jump when they heard a ship's horn. Turning around, they saw a coast guard boat chase after the other boat. Knowing they weren't completely out of danger, he hugged Evie tight. He didn't want to let go. Another coast guard boat came up and brought them aboard. They were quiet on the way back to the harbor but never left each other's side.

~*~

It was a long twenty-four hours. They spent the night talking to the police, then showing them where they found the body, and getting chewed out for not coming to them first. Evie was worried Jeremy would go out and move the body after the run in, but it seems he spent the night evading the coast guard. No one is sure exactly how he did it. After that, they made sure Kaitlin and Jake were reimbursed for the boat.

All Evie wanted to do was sleep for a day or two but Anthony was too paranoid about Jeremy knowing where they were. He was well-founded in his worry. They decided to book numerous flights leaving about the same time so that Jeremy wouldn't be sure which one they were on. They did the same thing in Ft. Lauderdale, all going to different parts of the country. Figuring that going back to Ipswich would be the most logical, they decided to go somewhere else.

As soon as they were in the air on their way to Seattle, Evie fell into a deep, dreamless sleep.

~*~

Jeremy tried to control his anger. The only thing that gave him solace was the fact they were running scared. He replayed the video of them making love as he slowly stroked himself, not coming just yet.

Switching to the video, he recorded while chasing them down, he moved his hand harder and faster seeing the fear on their faces. Freezing the frame when Evie came into view at the end with blood on her face, he finally had his release.

– CHAPTER FIFTEEN –

Traveling on the rutted road leading out to the Ellison house in the middle of nowhere, Evie was thankful for the sleep she got on the cross-country flight. They had a brief layover in San Francisco before getting into Seattle late, or really it was early in the morning. The extra security measures they had to take making sure it was Anthony, not Jeremy, made things more difficult. Even though they got a room, she tossed and turned for the rest of the night. The phone call home didn't help anything. It seemed that some of the security guards were refusing to guard the Troublesome Trio. Thankfully they hadn't done anything to them they just didn't like the comments or being treated like a piece of meat. Noah had to question all of the guards to see which ones would actually guard the Trio.

Later in the morning after their arrival she watched the dust in the side rearview mirror she wondered what they would find. The property was in Jay Ellison's name. Which meant the police didn't know about it. She felt sick to her stomach. This is where Jeremy grew up. After everything happened with Lexi, they found out more about Jeremy. Like the fact that his father killed his mother, most likely in that home in front of the nine-year-old boy. From the reports, they were able to find out that his parents didn't have a good relationship, but since his father was the Sherriff, no one would say anything. His mother found someone else and was going to leave both his father and him. Evie could have sympathy for the little boy, if it was true, to have your mom leave you with, from all accounts, a complete asshole. But on the other hand, what could have happened to flip that switch for him to become a serial killer? It couldn't be just the fact his mother was going to leave him and then Tiffani. Two women he loved not wanting him.

Jeremy's father started drinking more and more and he ended up losing his job. After the new Sherriff was in charge, a hiker found the body of his mother. They reopened the investigation into her death and found enough proof to put his father away. Twelve-year-old Jeremy was put in the system, moving from foster home to foster home. First, he got into a lot of trouble, but as he became more practiced, he started to fly under the radar.

"I've been thinking," Evie said.

"Now there's a scary thought."

She punched him in the shoulder. "Stop. About Jeremy. So his mother was going to leave him, then

Tiffani left him for you. Do you think that is what flipped his switch? If he really loved her like he told Lexi…"

"True, but sad to say, that happens to a lot of people, yet they never become serial killers."

Evie sighed, "I guess I'm just trying to get a handle on him. The more we know, the more we can figure out, the better chance we have to catch him."

Anthony reached over and grabbed her hand. "Have I thanked you yet for everything you're doing?"

"Nope."

He pulled over to the side of the road and turned to face her. "Truly, thank you. You've been in danger, almost killed, seen things you should've never seen. All to help. Quite frankly, it's shocking in this day and age that someone would pretty much drop everything to help someone they felt needed it, especially at the risk of injury to themselves." She looked away but he grabbed her chin. With their eyes locked together he continued, "Thank you."

She felt embarrassed under his scrutiny. "Really, there are more people out there that would help than you think."

"Then you have more faith in people than I do." He turned back and put the car in gear. They were quiet the rest of the short ride to the house.

Looking around Evie shuddered knowing at least one murder took place here. The vegetation was grown over, part of the roof was sinking in and windows were broken. Getting out of the car she looked around trying to see why someone would want to live out here so far from other people They hadn't seen another house in miles. It was a beautiful view, but maybe knowing what she knew is what made it seem dark.

The closer they got to the house, the worse the smell got. Looking at each other, they knew what was on the other side of that broken down door wasn't good.

Anthony reached out and offered his hand. "We go in together. We stay together." After she nodded he continued. "But if I tell you to get out, you get the hell out. Understood?"

Remembering the last time, she nodded again.

Taking a deep breath, they entered.

~*~

Another alarm went off on Jeremy's computer. Although there was no electricity at his old home he had a battery alarm system to notify him if someone stumbled onto it. Now he knew where they went, and what they were going to find. Cursing the fact he'd been unable to install cameras there, he sat back to think about what them finding it meant to him. Rage built within him until it boiled over. Systematically going through his room, he destroyed everything he could get his hands on. It wasn't the same as killing a woman, but it did take the edge off. Picking up his things, he tossed a couple hundred dollars on the bed and walked out of the room, never looking back.

~*~

Evie looked around in wonder. The front door opened to the living room. Pictures covered the walls. Getting a closer look she saw that most of them were old and she assumed of Jeremy's parents. They were so badly damaged, she couldn't be sure. It was hard to tell who got the most of his anger, his father or his mother. You could see where they were sliced and stabbed over and over, each and every one of them. The only person never marked was the little boy. As they walked around the room, you could see the little boy growing up and getting more and more distant. She lifted her hand and touched the little baby, an innocent little child who didn't know the hell that would happen to him in his young life.

She saw a happy smiling toddler. But even then you could see that he didn't smile as much if his father was near him. He clung to his mother. By the time she guessed he was around five, his expression was weary in every picture. The damage to the pictures became more violent as the boy grew up in them. She stopped at the last picture. This one had to be taken right before his mother was killed. She shivered, his eyes looked almost dead. So different from the smiling child he'd started as.

Seeing nothing amiss in the kitchen, they went to the first bedroom door and looked in. Evie gasped. You could tell it was a boy's room. Old football posters covered the walls, he was a 49ers fan. But the twin bed had, as far as she could tell, five skeletons on it.

Anthony walked into the room and started going through the dresser and closet, there was nothing in them.

She walked closer and counted six ribcages and no heads. "What did he do?" Her voice shook. "I don't see any heads on these skeletons."

"I have no idea. Come on. Let's see what else we can find."

"Shouldn't we call the police?" She shuddered. "There's got to be more."

"We will, after we finish looking around. You know they will lock this place up and we won't know for days, if not weeks, what they found."

"You're right. Let's get this over with."

The door at the end of the hall was partially open. Using his foot, Anthony pushed it all the way open to reveal the bathroom. It was worse than any horror movie she had ever seen. Blood covered every surface. The smell was disgusting. Thoughts whirled through her mind at what could have happened in here and she thought she might be sick.

They turned to the last room. Once again he used his foot to open the door all the way. This time Evie did throw-up. Turning away from Anthony she lost what little was in her stomach. He rubbed her back as it emptied. The image would not leave her head.

There tied to the bed was a decomposing body of a woman on top of a tarp, without a head and all of her flesh peeled off. The smell was overwhelming and even in her head she could still see the maggots moving over her.

"Fuck. Let's get out of here," Anthony said.

She could only nod and try to make her feet move down the hall. When they got back to the living room, they stopped. Anthony started looking around.

"What do you think he did with the heads?"

Evie shuddered. "I don't even want to think about that."

She followed as he moved back into the kitchen and started opening cabinets.

"What do you think he put them under the sink with the cleaning supplies?" She was starting to lose it.

"This was the only other place we didn't look through everything. Well, besides the last room."

He paused with one hand on each of the handles for the refrigerator. She saw him take a deep breath before he opened it. "Don't look."

But it was too late, she already saw. There were seven heads in there. Because there was no electricity the smell was horrific. It looked as if their faces were melting in there, dripping things down on the bottom of the refrigerator. With the door open, some of it spilled out onto the floor.

Evie was picked up and Anthony moved quickly out the front door into the sunlight. He sat her down on the hood of the car. Shivering so hard, she thought her teeth would break as they chattered against each other, she was thankful the engine had left the hood still warm. Watching the grass blow in the breeze, she stared without blinking.

She didn't acknowledge when Anthony put a shirt around her shoulders or when he climbed up behind her, wrapping his arms around her waist pulling her tight to him.

They stayed that way until Evie finally spoke. "It's going to be another long night at a police station isn't it."

"Looks like it."

"Why?" She knew she wasn't going to have to fill in the blanks, he knew what she was talking about.

"I have no idea. Obviously he holds them responsible and because he grew up here, no matter how bad it was, it's still a 'safe' place for him."

"But to keep the decapitated heads in the fridge? Really?" Her eyes grew huge and a laugh escaped her lips. "Oh my god."

"What?"

"I've always loved Halloween." She giggled. "And every year…" She tried to control the laughter that was starting to bubble up. "I always put de…" Another laugh came out. "Fake decapitated heads in the fridge to scare people." She completely lost it and couldn't stop the laughter or the tears that started falling. Holding onto Anthony's hands as he rocked her, she laughed and cried for the women inside the house.

~*~

It was a long couple of days. They spent hours talking to the police before they were finally able to get a room, clean up, and get some sleep. Everything Anthony had seen kept replaying in his head. Between that and the nightmares Evie had, he wasn't sure he got any sleep. He held onto her as she clung to him most of the night. He was both scared and felt bad for her every time she screamed.

The next day they'd talked to anyone who'd known Jeremy and his parents. They didn't learn much more than they already knew. But as Evie always said, every little bit will help put the whole puzzle together.

He was looking forward to getting together with Noah so they could analyze the new information. He looked over at Evie in the light of the setting sun on the drive to catch their plane to go back to Ipswich, wishing he could keep the women out of it, knowing it would be impossible. He could see the strain of everything that had been going on in Evie's eyes. He wanted to bring light back into them. Once this was all over, and Jeremy was caught, he'd do just that.

~*~

Since Anthony and Evie were all the way across country, Jeremy decided to head back to where he knew they would end up eventually. Smiling at his luck, he couldn't believe it. The old bat was home alone. He'd made sure Evie's stupid brother went down to the city for the night. The only person he'd have to worry about was the guard. It was surprisingly easy to sneak up behind him and slice his neck open. Looking down, he tilted his head to the side. The knife didn't cut as deeply as he'd hoped. He was going to have to sharpen it before he used it next.

After going through the cottage and finding nothing, he moved towards the main house. Silently creeping through, he arrived at Evie's bedroom. He was disappointed there was no dirty laundry for him to go through. He went over to the bed and pulled the covers back. Slowly leaning down he moved from the top of the bed to the bottom smelling, closing his eyes in appreciation of the fact the linens on the bed had not been washed since she'd been gone.

He could smell her on them. This was the closest he'd ever been to her. He'd been missing out on her scent. His cock pulsated with anticipation. He pulled his pants down and slid up the bed on his stomach, burying his face in her pillow. He imagined he was pounding his cock hard and fast into her wet pussy. He thought of it being extra wet with all the blood.

Biting down as hard as he could on her pillow, imagining it being her neck, he thrashed his head back and forth, thinking of ripping the flesh off. That last thought was all it took to push him over the edge and he emptied himself all over her sheets. He rolled over and rubbed it into the sheets.

Pulling his pants back up, he took one last look at the room. A spur of the moment decision had him going back to her dresser and pulling out a couple pair of panties. Putting them in his pocket he walked to the next room. Silently opening the door, he walked in as if he owned the place. When he got to the side of the bed, he looked down at the sleeping old woman. She had no idea he was there, no idea what was coming.

– CHAPTER SIXTEEN –

E vie sighed and relaxed against the seat in the car on the way back to her grandmother's house. The red-eye from Seattle was uneventful, except she didn't get much sleep. The nightmares weren't as frequent as the first night, but she didn't want to panic the whole plane by waking up screaming.

She was hopeful that with the new information they just received they might be able to get somewhere. Anthony's friend had come through and they'd found the flight information. It was a long shot, and a lot of names to go through, but maybe something would show up. It couldn't be as easy as Jay Ellison was on a flight to a murder site around the time one happened.

Gasping, Evie sat up and leaned forward in her seat to get a better view out of the windshield. There were police cars and crime scene tape all around her grandmother's house. Frantically searching the crowd she couldn't see anyone she knew. As soon as Anthony stopped the car, she was out and running towards the house screaming her grandmother's name.

Strong arms grabbed her from behind and held her from going any further. Kicking and squirming to get out of his hold, she turned and started beating her fists on his chest. "Let me go! I've got to get to Grams!"

"Miss Taylor?"

Evie turned around; the police officer was so serious. Thoughts whirled in her head. This couldn't be good. *Please God, let her be ok.* She nodded, not able to form words. Starting to feel lightheaded because she was breathing so fast, she leaned back into Anthony searching for his strength. She took small comfort as his arms wrapped tightly around her.

"There was a break-in here last night."

Evie's hand flew to her mouth. "Oh no." Everything started to spin. She was having a hard time concentrating on his words.

Anthony leaned down and whispered in her ear. "You're stronger than this. Calm down."

His words seeped into her soul and she grabbed onto them. "Tell me."

"A, Jackson Taylor, came home a little bit ago; it appears he went down to Boston for the night. When your grandmother wasn't downstairs as he expected he went upstairs looking for her. She was gagged and tied to the bed. They took her to the hospital to get checked out, but she should be fine. The guard on the other hand, didn't make it."

Evie sagged against Anthony, almost bringing them both down in the process. "She's okay. She's okay. I've got to get to her." She pushed out of his arms and started running to the car. When he didn't follow, she turned back around. "Come on."

"I'll be there in a minute. I just have a couple of questions."

"You've got two minutes; otherwise I'm stealing your car."

"La mia belezza, you might not want to say that in front of the officer."

Fuming, she flung herself in the car. Tears started falling and she buried her face in her hands. She'd been so scared that her grandmother was dead. She should've never left her here alone. They should have made sure security was here for her. Her anger towards her brother intensified. She couldn't wait to see him, wanting to kick his ass for leaving her there alone.

Looking up when Anthony opened the door, she felt like his calm was the only thing keeping her in control. When he pulled her into a hug, she didn't notice the gearshift digging into her side. His warmth and support filled her up, making her feel halfway normal again. When he let her go, she leaned back into her seat. "Drive and talk. What did you find out?"

"It was Jeremy."

"Shit."

"He left a message. He wanted to make sure we got it."

"And, what was it."

"He told your grandmother that he could get to you any time he wanted. You'd never be safe. He's planning on making this kill like no other."

Evie shuddered thinking back to what they found in New York and at his childhood home. "That can't be good."

"No, it's not. So some things are going to change."

"If you are thinking what I think you're thinking you can just stop now. We'll argue about this later."

"Yes, we will."

As soon as the car was stopped she ran towards the door. Anthony caught her quickly even with her head start. After finding out which floor her grandmother was on, she waited impatiently for the elevator. "Maybe we should take the stairs?"

"You don't want to be all out of breath when you get to her room do you?"

Crossing her arms across her chest, she started to tap her foot. She would've run over the people waiting to get out if Anthony hadn't grabbed her and held her back.

All she wanted to do was see her grandmother, to make sure she was really okay. Walking quickly down the hall, the first person she saw was her brother leaning against the wall looking down at his feet. Needing to lash out at someone she went up to him and punched him in the gut. "You bastard," she hissed trying to keep her voice down. "How could you leave her alone? You know Jeremy is still out there. What?

Did you have the urge to stick your dick in some willing pussy for the night? It couldn't wait?"

"Ease up, Evie. It's not like that." Jackson ran his fingers through his hair.

"Start talking. Now, asshat."

Sighing, he dropped his hands to his side. "I got a call from a guy I knew in Boston. He had a line on some information about Jeremy being in Boston."

"So what, you just dropped everything and went down there? What were you thinking?"

"Gee, I don't know, what would you have done? I love Lexi, too, you know. And now with you running all over the place trying to find Jeremy, I don't want to lose you, too. I can't just sit around and do nothing. Besides, the guard was with her."

Evie closed her eyes. She knew what she would have done. The same thing. "Fine. Did you learn anything?"

"No, I spent all night going from one place to the other with nothing. It seems like it might have been a set up to get me out of the house."

Wanting to purr like a cat, when Anthony started rubbing her back she held back. "Well, we know why he wanted you out of the house. Just next time make sure there is more than just one other person there with her."

Anthony cleared his throat. "That is part of what we are going to be arguing about later."

She could have laughed at the confused expression on her brother's face. "Great. Now I've got to see Grams."

Rushing to the side of her bed, Evie looked her grandmother over from head to toe. Seeing that she was really okay she grabbed her and gave her a hug. "You scared me so bad."

"I'm fine, honey. It was scary when he was there. I didn't know what he was going to do. But after he left I just got pissed off. Now if I ever see him again, I'm going to rip his dick off and put it in a meat grinder. Then I'm going to pour lemon juice all over it, then…"

Anthony held up his hand to make her stop. "I think we get the idea."

"He's just lucky he caught me while I was sleeping. Otherwise, his dick would be mine."

"I think we've got it. Now how much longer do you have to be here?"

"Depends on when Dr. McHottness springs me. If he'd give me sponge baths, I'd stay here forever."

Evie leaned down and kissed her forehead. "You'd ruin him for all other women."

"Damn-skippy I would. Once you have a taste of me, no other woman will leave you as satisfied."

"Where's Leigh and Marie?" Evie looked around starting to get worried. While no direct relation to her and Lexi, they still meant a lot to them.

"Don't worry; they just went down to see if there were any cute guys in the cafeteria. They're trying to get some to come and cheer me up."

"I'm sure they're doing all that they can. Why don't we go down there and hurry them up?" Evie was scared of what kind of trouble they could be getting into. She could see them getting banned from the hospital.

Anthony took the time to call Noah while Evie was dealing with the other ladies. He was amazed how much trouble they could get into. Seems there was an incident with whipped cream and a young man.

With everything set up, he knew he had to let the others in on his plan. Hoping it wouldn't be too much of a fight, he decided to talk to Evie and her grandmother while they were on their way back to the house.

"Ladies, when we get back I want you both to pack a bag. You'll be staying with Noah and Lexi until Jeremy is caught." He gripped the steering wheel waiting for what would happen next.

"Hell no. We aren't hiding away like some weak women who need protecting by men," Evie said turning angry eyes to him.

"No one kicks me out of my house."

"It's not like that. We figure if everyone is under one roof, with a wall around the property and security patrolling, not to mention the alarm, everyone will be safe."

Evie crossed her arms and narrowed her eyes at him. "Everyone?"

"Well, you, your grandmother, Jackson, Marie and Leigh."

"What about you?"

"I'll be around."

"But not staying there."

"No, I don't think it would be good for Lexi. Noah agreed."

"So what you are left out there alone with no protection? I'll say it again, *hell no*. I'll stay with you."

Sighing, he knew she was going to be like this. "La mia belezza, think about it. You wouldn't be safe."

"Don't you go all sweet talking me, *you* wouldn't be safe out there alone."

"Yes, I will. He doesn't want to physically do anything to me. He wants to make sure I mentally suffer. I'm safe."

Shaking her head at him she said, "No, you don't get it. Think about it. He somehow captures you. I get a phone call from him saying he has you. I'd do anything I could to find you. Then he'd find me. Don't you think he'd enjoy killing me in front of you? Making you watch the whole thing without being able to do anything to save me?"

He knew she had a point. Maybe he could stay in Lexi's old house. They were using it as a guest house now but no one was there. They wanted everyone up at the main house, together.

"I'll see if I could stay in Lexi's old house."

"See? Now we're talking. I'm still pissed about the whole thing, but if you're there I'll feel better."

"I won't," Evelyne said from the backseat. "We have our house and things to do there. I don't want to impose. How long do you think we'll be there? What if its years?"

"It can't be that long. We all need him to be caught so that we can get on with our lives." Anthony said as he glanced at Evie.

"Have you talked to Leigh and Marie?"

"Noah said he'd have Lexi do it. He texted me. They're on board."

Pulling into the driveway at Evelyne's house he turned to them. "Please, let's do this, at least for now. Besides, we all need to go over a lot of information. Maybe something will come of it."

Evelyne leaned forward so that her head was between theirs. "Do we get secret agent names? Can I be Hot Snatch?"

Anthony was so happy nothing really bad happened to her. You never knew what was going to come out of her mouth. It was a refreshing change to be around women who spoke their mind, even if some of the things on them were a bit disturbing, especially considering their age.

He watched Evie lean over and kiss her grandma's cheek. "You can be whoever you want." The love and devotion she had for her family and friends was something he admired.

"Okay, ladies, let's get your stuff and get out of here. I want to make sure we are to Noah's before dark." As they approached the front door he asked,

"Do I need to rent a truck so that we can get all your stuff over there?"

He was rewarded by a backhand to his stomach from Evie. Smiling, he was happy his plans were working out so well.

~*~

After everyone was settled into their rooms, they all met in the kitchen to snack on the food that Martha put out for them. Sam was mysteriously absent. Evie felt it had to do with the fact the Troublesome Trio was in the house. She felt bad, knowing the next days or weeks were going to be hard on him. Lucky for him, there were young, built security guards all over the place. They all knew the score and most of them had fun with the ladies. The ones that didn't were scheduled to work along the wall.

There were papers and food spread over every flat surface in the area. Anthony and Evie brought everyone up to date with what they had found. They spent hours going over ideas and looking through paperwork. Everyone had lists of flight manifests. There were more than anyone thought.

Needing to rest her eyes, Evie walked over and sat on the edge of the couch next to her grandmother. "What are you whispering about over here?"

"I have no idea what you could be talking about," Marie said as she smoothed the wrinkles on her pants.

Giving them a look, she crossed her legs and rested her chin on her hand. "I'm waiting. Come on, I'm tired and stressed, just spill it."

"Oh, honey, you should get some sleep." Leigh said. When Evie didn't reply, she continued, "Fine, we were just commenting on the hotties in the room."

"Well, I was commenting on two of them." Evelyne pointed over her shoulder. "These two horn dogs were going all out."

"And what conclusions did you come to?"

Leigh was vibrating with excitement and scooted to the edge of the sofa. "Well, it's like this. We figure we've got a great cross-section of men. First you have Noah, rock and roll all the way, bad boy and tattooed. Then you have Anthony, tall, built, and my god, that man could be a supermodel. Then you add the company and money he has, superhot. Then there's Jackson, the all-American boy next door, loyal, and can make you laugh. See, they're all there." Leigh waved her hand over to where the three of them stood together looking at a map.

Evie couldn't disagree. They all were handsome, although her brother she saw as more of a pain in the ass than anything else. She looked over to where Lexi was sitting, keeping her distance from Anthony, but the more they were together, the more she loosened up.

Lexi noticed her watching and said, "Either I'm more tired than I realize or I'm seeing the same name everywhere."

Evie got up and walked over to her. "Which ones?"

"This one. David Waters."

Evie sat there and thought for a moment, someone tried to talk and she shushed them. She was trying to remember something. Snapping her fingers together she ran back over to where she'd been going through papers. Flipping through them, she found what she was looking for. Then she went on to another two, and sure enough there it was. "Here. He's been on all of these flights. It can't be a coincidence. Can it?"

Anthony walked over to her and gave her a hug. She caught Lexi staring at them and knew there would be questions later.

Everyone started searching their packets and ended up with three more.

Both Anthony and Noah got on the phone to their people asking them to search for anything on this David Waters. There was an excitement in the air. Maybe this was the break they needed.

Evie started pacing the room. Wanting answers, she went over to the laptop and started her own search, hoping that would help time go by faster. Anthony and Noah sat down at their laptops, checking to see if they had any new mail. When one of theirs finally dinged the room became hushed.

It was Anthony's. Evie moved her chair closer so that she could see his screen better waiting for him to check it.

"That had better not be spam for male enhancement," said Evelyne.

"Not to worry, ladies, it's from my investigator." He was silent as he read. Evie would have hit him if she wasn't able to read with him.

When he got to the end he opened the attachment that had a copy of his passport picture. It was Jeremy.

They sent the Trio and Lexi off to bed while the rest of them went through the information. David Waters didn't own much, or have any debt. In fact, there was only one thing he owned. A home in La Jolla.

Evie leaned back in her chair. "Well, we know where we are going next."

Anthony looked at her. "There is no 'we,' it's me. You stay here."

"Like hell I am. We're in this together."

"Haven't you been paying attention? It isn't safe for you."

"I can take care of myself. Listen here, buddy…"

"Time out," Jackson said. "While I agree Evie should stay here…" He held her off as she jumped him. "Let me finish. You know there is no way she'll stay here. Might as well take her with us so we can keep an eye on her."

"Us? What you're inviting yourself?" Evie snarled at him.

"Yes, I think the more men, the better."

"I should go, too." Noah said. "I'd love to get my hands on that bastard for what he did to Lexi."

Evie walked over to him. Placing her hands on his face so that he'd look at her she said, "No, Noah. You have to stay here with Lexi. She's yours now. Her and that little baby she's carrying. You know she doesn't need the extra stress of worrying about you. If it makes you feel better, I'll kick him in the nuts a few times for you."

He pulled her into a hug. "You'd better. I know you're right, but it feels like I'm taking the easy way out."

Jackson laughed. "Easy way? Buddy, you're stuck here with a pregnant woman and the Trio. You are more screwed than we are."

"Shit. You might be right. But you can't go by yourselves. I think you should take someone who is trained in security with you." Before Evie could argue, Noah stopped her. "You know it will make Lexi rest easier knowing someone will be with you."

"Fine."

"Why is it when women say fine it's really a 'fuck you' or 'asshole?'" Noah asked.

"Because it is. Okay, which brute is coming with us? What about that big scary one who never smiles and lurks around in the shadows?"

"I heard that," said a voice from the other room.

"You were supposed to!" Evie shouted.

Shaking his head, Noah continued. "I'm thinking Kat would be the best."

"Why Kat? Won't Lexi need her?"

"Couple of reasons. One of these two guys can't be with you all the time." Seeing her nod, he knew she'd commit now. "And Lexi doesn't need to go anywhere for two weeks. Plenty of time for you guys to go out there and see what you can find before we turn this information over to the police."

"Oh man, she's not going to like that."

"I know, but I'll take my punishment like a man." He winked and walked out of the room.

She looked at Anthony. "So, another trip."

"So it would seem."

"I'll look for flights."

He pulled her into a hug. "One of these days we are going to go on a trip for fun. Not to chase a sick bastard."

"I'll hold you to that."

"I know you will."

~*~

"No!" Jeremy screamed. They knew everything. They were going to find everything. Travel had become very hard for him. There was no way that he would make it out to La Jolla before they got there. He lay back on the bed, staring up at the ceiling wondering what he was going to do now.

All his precious pictures, they were going to be gone. He'd never be able to go back there. His chest constricted. They couldn't take that from him now, there would be hell to pay.

~*~

Evie knew exactly where she was going and what she was doing. She was banking on the fact that Lexi would still have a key hidden in the same spot of the cottage. Sure enough it was still there. Letting herself in she surprised Anthony as he was sitting at the kitchen table. He jumped up and stalked over to her stopping just inches from her.

"What in the hell are you doing? Are you crazy? Did you walk over here by yourself? What were you thinking?"

"Which question would you like for me to answer first?"

Through gritted teeth he said, "Pick one."

"No, I am not crazy. Yes, I walked over here by myself. But before you go all caveman on me I let one of the security guards know I was coming over." She started to flip the porch light on and off three times. "But if I didn't do that within five minutes he was coming over. As to why I am here, well, besides *liking* to spend time with you, I've grown used to sleeping in the same bed with you. And I wouldn't put it past you to find some way to leave without me." She crossed her arms.

Suddenly, she was enveloped in his arms. "Don't you ever scare me like that again. What if something had happened? You could have been gone and no one would have known."

"Yes they would have, within five minutes."

"You could be dead in five minutes. Don't ever do that again. Call me, I'll come get you. Or at least have one of the guards walk over with you. Please."

Seeing the fear in his eyes she hated the fact she had put it there. "I promise."

– CHAPTER SEVENTEEN –

Evie knew it was only a matter of time before Lexi pulled her aside and talked to her about Anthony. They were on the back patio overlooking the ocean.

"Do you want to tell me what is going on?" Lexi demanded.

"What do you mean?" Evie's stomach dropped.

"Come on, I'm not stupid. Spill. What's up with you and Anthony?"

"He's not Jeremy."

"I know that." Lexi sighed. "But I don't think I like what I see."

"And what is it that you see?"

"Really? Are you going to make me say it? I know you went over there last night. I know you were there *all* night long. Are you fucking him?"

"So what if I am? *He's* not Jeremy. There is so much more to him. I can't deny the pull he has on me. I can't stay away."

"I knew it! How could you do this? Do you understand what this means? Some sicko has you in his sights now. It was bad enough when it was just me, now it's you, too. Do you understand what he is going to do to you? He will make sure you hurt." Lexi's voice wavered. "It's like a pain you've never felt before." She grabbed Evie by the arms. "You know I still have nightmares? Hell, so does Noah. This isn't something that just goes away with a snap of a finger. It takes time. It will always be with me. Do you think I want that for you?"

"I know what I'm doing."

"You're going to get hurt. I don't want that to happen to you. You've got to back away from him. I wish you weren't going. Please stay here."

"I can't. I've got to go." Evie dropped her arms to her side. "I wish I could explain it to you." She walked over and sat down on the low wall. "You know I'll do anything for my family and friends, it starts there. With you. I can help. I know I can. I want that bastard caught so that you can at least feel a little safer. I want to take your nightmares away. And all the other women. There are so many. I want to protect them, too. The nameless women out there who don't know, but might be next on his list. They don't deserve it any more than the women who came before."

Evie stood up and started pacing. "Then there is Anthony. He's had so much happen to him that isn't his fault. But even after all of that he's got such a determination to find this bastard, to see things through. And all the time still take care of his business and his friends. Just *friends* because this monster took his only family. He's alone out there trying to fight for justice."

Evie walked over to stand behind Lexi and wrap her arms around her resting her chin on top of her head. "Lexi, he's my shelter. When everything is going crazy around us like some wicked storm, when I'm with him it's like everything is calm. It's like we're in the eye of the storm, everything is swirling and blowing around us, but the sun is shining and there's blue skies when I'm in his arms, safe. I can see and think more clearly with him around. He's my rock."

Lexi sighed. "I don't like it."

Evie moved so she could look at Lexi. "What exactly is it you don't like? The fact he looks like Jeremy or the fact I might get hurt."

"Both. I know he's not Jeremy and really after spending time with him I can see the differences. Trust me; my last encounter with Jeremy is something I'm not forgetting anytime soon. It still takes me back a little every time I see him, but after a few minutes I know it's not Jeremy, it's Anthony. But I'm so afraid that Jeremy's going to get you and kill you. I don't know if I could handle that."

"I'm scared, too, but you know hiding isn't something I can do. Look at you. How much did you frustrate people with your need for independence? Hello! Like everyone. I need to see this through, not just for you, but for Anthony, too."

"I know. Please be careful. Come back to me."

"I will, and hopefully with some answers."

~*~

Evie looked over at Kat driving them to the address they had for the only thing Jeremy owned under the name of David Waters, not sure what was going on with her. Kat had never been overly warm, but there were times when she seemed to open up a little bit with Lexi and Evie over the past year. She remembered the one time Kat had really opened up to them. They'd been trying on swimsuits for the summer. They had fun picking out the funniest ones they could find and trying them on. Since Lexi loved the water and Kat would be spending time with her, she needed one, too. They all had tears running down their faces from laughing so hard.

It was like looking at someone completely different now. She wanted nothing to do with Anthony or Jackson. That was really unusual. Jackson always had women falling over him, and Anthony, well, he was just so gorgeous. But she could understand the hesitation there since Jeremy looked so much like him. Kat had made sure that she sat by herself on the plane. She didn't want to sit near anyone, nor was she really talking.

They drove through the gates and up to a large house on the bluffs overlooking the ocean in La Jolla. A beautiful setting she knew hid a deep and dark secret. Would it hold what they were all wondering about? She didn't ask any questions of Anthony on how they were getting access. She figured the less she knew, better.

They all had gloves on as they approached the house and Anthony pushed the buttons on the keypad somehow one of his men had gotten for them and that let them in. At some point, she knew they were going to get into trouble for finding evidence and not turning it over to the police first, but they wanted as much information as they could.

Spending hours going through the house and finding nothing, they finally ended their search in his bedroom. The view was spectacular from here. Evie was distracted by the view and the thoughts that were whirling through her head didn't notice anything out of the ordinary until Jackson said something to Anthony. Turning around, she saw Anthony looking at the wall then he would go out of the bedroom, walk into the master bathroom and closet, and then do it all over again.

"What are you doing?" she asked.

"Something is off. There seems to be something missing."

"What do you mean?"

"Look, the only thing on the other side of this wall is his closet and bathroom, yet they are both smaller than they should be." He grabbed her hand and they both started to pace it off. Sure enough either the closet or master bath should have been larger. They looked at each other their eyes filled with excitement.

"You start in the bathroom, I'll take the closet." She whirled from him and went into the closet looking at the back wall that should have been shared with the master bath. Running her hand along it with Jackson on the other side of her they started searching for anything that might be a release.

"Are you going to help Kat?" Evie called to her.

"No."

After a few minutes of searching, she felt something different at the back of the drawers that were on the wall. It felt like a button. "Guys, I think I've got something." She pressed the button and heard a click, the wall in question started to slowly open. "Anthony!"

The three of them pushed forward to go into a small room. Evie felt like she was going to be sick. Photos covered the walls. Women in all sorts of torture and pain. There were so many of them. She didn't want to look at the ones of Lexi. She knew what she had been through, had seen her right after, but seeing it being done to her was something else. She focused on the other women. Putting names to faces. There was Tiffani, Natalie, Monique, Chelle, and Heather. Not to mention the others she could only assume were of the women they found at his childhood home.

She heard a whimper behind her and turned to see Kat standing there with tears running down her face staring at the photos on the wall. Evie turned back around to see which ones she was looking at. Tilting her head, she moved forward to get a closer look. Kat had been looking at the pictures of Chelle Michaels. Getting closer Evie saw a naked woman stretched out on a bed before Jeremy had started hurting her. Evie's eyes widened. *It couldn't be.* She turned and looked at Kat. Seeing the expression on her face, she knew it must be.

Chelle Michaels and Kat Snyder had the same birthmark on their stomach. The same birthmark Evie had noticed when they had been trying on swimsuits a few months ago.

– CHAPTER EIGHTEEN –

"You bitch." Evie screamed as she launched herself at Kat. Strong arms came around her and lifted her up off of the ground. "Let me go, Anthony, I don't want to hurt *you*."

"What the fuck is going on?" he hissed in her ear.

Still wiggling to get out of his hold she said, "That bitch over there is Chelle Michaels. You know one of the women we thought was *dead*. She's known all along. She's been protecting Lexi. She never said a word!"

Kat started to back out of the room. Jackson walked over behind her effectively making it so she couldn't leave.

"Maybe you should explain how you came to that conclusion Evie," Jackson said calmly.

"Kat has the exact same birthmark as Chelle on her stomach. I've seen it. See?" She pointed to the picture. "It's one of those large red ones. I noticed because it looks like a cat. I thought it was interesting that her name was Kat. Now I see a picture of Chelle, and she has the *exact same one!*"

"Do you have anything to say Kat?" Anthony asked.

"No."

"Well you'd better start talking and fast otherwise does obstruction of justice mean anything to you?" Venom filled Evie's words.

"How the hell do we know she isn't working with Jeremy? How else would he always know what we were planning to do? It's her! She's telling him everything." Evie screamed at Kat.

Kat's tears were flowing faster. "No, no, no, no. I'd never have anything to do with that bastard. I want him found, I want him to suffer. I want him dead like I've wanted nothing else in my life." She looked to the men. "You've got to believe me. There is no way I'd be associated with that bastard." She stared into Jackson's eyes. "Please. Please believe me. I don't want anyone hurt but him."

"I believe her," Jackson said.

"What are you crazy? She could be making this all up. No way is she getting anywhere near Lexi. Fuck no."

"Evie, calm down. Think with your head. If she was going to harm Lexi, wouldn't she have done it months ago?" Seeing his sister's stubborn look he continued. "Why don't we just listen to her story, and then decide what to do?"

Kat shook her head, "I only want to tell my story once. Can we please just go back to Noah's? I'll tell everything then."

"You'd better tell us everything, otherwise what Jeremy did to you will be nothing like what I will. And you'd better not get within ten feet of Lexi." Evie finally got out of Anthony's hold and pushed past Kat.

They decided not to let the police know what they found until after everyone heard Kat's story. To stay one step ahead of Jeremy they wanted everything they could find out before letting the authorities know. They took photos on their cell phones so that they had them to reference back to later. They were lucky and were able to get a flight out within a few hours. It was a long trip back across the country. Anthony couldn't believe everything they had found and discovered. Kat was actually Chelle Michaels. She seemed so different now than the teacher he had met in Los Angeles all those years ago.

Trying to piece together what he knew about that case and Kat he was coming up with blanks. He wanted to press her for information but she had refused to answer any questions. She had allowed Jackson to sit by her but she just looked out the window, crying, not saying a word.

If she had recovered enough by the time Lexi was attacked the first time, she might have seen something that could've proven his innocence then, and he would have never gone to prison. They could have been looking for Jeremy years ago, not just now.

He felt his anger building. Maybe Lexi didn't even have to be attacked the second time. Maybe those other women didn't have to die. How could she not say anything?

His sense of justice was growing to where all he could think about was ending this bastard's life so everyone would be safe.

Lost in thought, the next thing he knew the captain came on saying they were preparing for descent. Making sure his and Evie's seatbelts were secured he waited to land, knowing a storm was brewing and wondering who was going to come out of it alive.

~*~

Once again, they were all gathered in the great room of Noah's house. The atmosphere was tense with only four of them knowing what was found and the rest wondering why they looked so angry.

Evie pulled Noah aside. "You'll want to stick by Lexi."

"Why? What's going on?"

Glaring at Kat, she debated letting Noah know before everyone else. "Well, let me put it to you this way. Kat isn't who she says she is and knows more than she ever let on."

Noah grabbed Evie by the arm. "Tell me."

Shaking her head she said, "I don't know much more than that. Kat said she wanted to tell everyone at once. I don't think it's good; Lexi is going to need you. And you might need to find a new bodyguard."

"Shit."

"Yeah. Come on, let's get some information."

Evie walked over to Anthony. She knew she was going to need to lean on him, and hopefully he would lean on her. Dreading what was coming, they sat down to hear Kat's story.

– CHAPTER NINETEEN –

Kat twisted her fingers together, she didn't want to do this. She'd hoped she'd never have to tell these people what had happened to her and what she had to do. Hoping she could get through to them and they wouldn't hate her, she accepted the glass of water Jackson handed her. He was the only one who wasn't openly hostile towards her. She didn't understand it but decided she'd take it.

Looking around the room at the people she'd spent so much time with the past year, she couldn't help but have feelings for them. They were always so nice to her and treated her more like a friend than employee. Spending most of her time trying to keep them at arm's length hadn't worked; somehow they'd found a place in her heart.

Taking a deep breath, she knew she couldn't put it off any longer. "I'm originally from Pittsburg. My family had always been into doing something to give back. Most of them were either police officers or fire fighters. But so many years ago, I was a first grade teacher. That was all I ever wanted. To teach children. To be around children. I wanted to fall in love and have a dozen of them. We were all a really close knit family, getting the whole gang together every weekend. They would all trade stories on catching the bad guy, making him pay or saving families from burning buildings. It was perfect."

Kat kept her eyes down, looking at her fingers. She didn't want to see the look in their eyes. She was sure some of them started to realize what was coming. "I had a great opportunity to go out to Los Angles. It was a teaching conference, the newest and best teaching tools to help kids. I remember wanting to go so badly. I had some kids that were having a really tough time. They didn't have the best home life and I wanted to help them. I knew an education was the only way for them to break out of the cycle. I wanted to help them. That's all I ever wanted was to help children. To have children."

She was surprised when Jackson came over and sat down next to her. While she didn't want to admit it, it helped knowing that maybe someone would, at least, listen to her. She hoped he wouldn't judge too hard.

"So in L.A. the hotel double booked my room." She nodded towards Anthony. "He was a gentleman. And so handsome. I have to admit I was hoping for a fairytale ending. You know, like something from a movie." She paused. "But that didn't happen. In fact, the opposite happened."

"No." whispered Lexi.

Kat looked up at her. "Yes. I was attacked and left for dead. I wanted to die. That was the only thing I knew when I woke up. But by that time my family was there, they swooped in and covered everything up. They didn't want him to know I was alive. They had everything sealed and moved me back to heal. It took a while. Then they told me I could never have children. He took that away from me. The only thing I ever really wanted in life, and it was ripped from me. I couldn't go back to teaching; I couldn't face all those children. Children whose parents treated them terribly, who didn't appreciate the miracle they had in their hands." She clenched her hands into fists when she saw how much they were shaking.

"I had some money so I told my family I had to leave. While the attack didn't happen there, it was too much. Seeing family and friends with babies, I couldn't take it. I took what I'd learned from my family about law enforcement and online courses and started tracking Anthony. I changed my name and my attitude. I wanted him to suffer as much as I had."

Looking over at Anthony she said, "I'm sorry. I hated you for so long. All that time looking in the wrong direction until one night. It was after your first date with Lexi. I noticed someone else watching. I couldn't believe my eyes. He looked so much like you. If I couldn't turn my head and see you I would never have believed it. I followed him; he must have known something was up because I lost him. I split my time between following Anthony and Lexi. I knew he'd have to show up at some point. I was there that night Lexi was attacked. I was pretty sure it wasn't Anthony, but I couldn't be sure. This time I was able to follow him to the airport where he boarded a flight to somewhere in the northwest. I couldn't get on the flight so I went back to see what Anthony was up to. That was when I learned about Lexi's attack. I couldn't believe what had happened while I was sitting there watching from outside."

"And you said nothing," Noah said.

"No, I didn't. I didn't have enough information."

"What about later? Obviously, at some point you knew more." Noah stood up and started towards her. "Tell us the rest. Now."

"As you already know, he disappeared while Anthony was in prison. I couldn't find him. So I focused on Lexi. I figured he might come back for her at some point."

"I never saw you, all those years." Lexi said in a small voice.

"I always dressed up with the kids, so I was in disguises a lot. I couldn't believe how lucky I was when he finally did show up. I almost had him so many times, but he'd always escape. It's like that bastard has nine lives or something."

Evie was on her feet stalking towards Kat. "You just sat back and let Lexi be attacked for the second time. After everything you've been through, how could you let him do that to another women?" Evie tried to shake off Anthony's grasp. "Do you understand what you've done? How many woman have died because you were so hung up on your own revenge you didn't say anything to anyone? Hell, my grandmother was almost killed!" Poking a finger into Kat's chest, "That's all on you. You talk about all you wanted was kids, well, what about those kids who have lost their mothers because you wouldn't say anything? What about that?"

Kat was crying, her head hanging down. "I know. I was obsessed. I wanted nothing more than making him pay. Make him suffer for taking my chance to have children away from me."

"Why? Why didn't you say anything sooner? Lexi didn't have to be attacked again. Hell, Anthony might not have ended up in prison! You could have been helping us. Instead you just stood there, doing *nothing*," Evie screamed at her.

Kat stood up and got in Evie's face. "Don't you think I'm living with that every single day of my life? Not just what he took from me, but everyone else. He needs to pay and I want to be the one to make him suffer. I want to hurt him just as much as he's hurt all these other women. I want him to beg for his life as I slowly kill him. I want my face to be the last he ever sees." Exhausted, she sat back down on the chair.

Kat sat there while everyone started talking at once. Everyone knew now, there was nothing left to hide. Well, just one thing. She looked over at Jackson.

~*~

Evie followed Lexi into the kitchen when everyone started arguing with each other on what to do next. "How are you doing?"

"I don't know. I can't believe she's been this close to me this whole time and never said anything." She rubbed a hand over her belly. "And now that I'm pregnant, I can't even begin to know what she has been feeling."

"What about the fact she's been lying?"

"It's easier for you to hold onto the anger. You forget I've been where she's been. I can completely understand where she's coming from."

"So what you're saying it's okay what she did?"

"No, I'm saying I understand. She was tortured, almost killed, and can't have children. The first two alone can change a person, but you add the third and yeah, I can understand."

"You're going all soft on me."

"No, just trying to show some compassion. I'm not saying I still want her as my bodyguard. I still think she is more interested in killing Jeremy than protecting me, but that also means I'm not going to kick her out on the street."

At the raised voices in the other room Evie pointed to them, "Well, you might want to tell your husband that. He's going all crazy rock star over there."

Evie leaned back against the counter and watched her pregnant best friend wade into the middle of three men who were all yelling at each other on what was the best course of action. She looked over at Kat who sat there looking at the floor, shoulders hunched. *The pain she must have gone through. Damn it Lexi, now she's got me going all soft.*

– CHAPTER TWENTY –

Kat got up and walked out of the house, unnoticed, or so she thought. She stood there and watched the ocean roll in. Wrapping her arms around herself she wondered how she got here. Wishing for the woman she used to be and not knowing how to get her back.

She stiffened when she heard someone come up behind her. Without looking, she knew who it was. "I'm not going anywhere."

Jackson was just inches behind her. She could feel his heat. "I know. I thought you could use a friend."

She whirled on him. "Why? I don't understand you."

He gently tucked a strand of hair behind her ear. "You never did." He held out his hand waiting for her to trust him. After a moment, she placed her hand in his and they walked back into the house.

~*~

Everyone was up early and watching the news when Anthony and Evie walked in. They had decided to call the authorities last night and it was all over the news about Jeremy Ellison and his horrific crimes. It was nothing compared to what had been on last time after he attacked Lexi. Now with all the new information from New York, London, St. Thomas, Seattle and La Jolla, there was no hiding what he had done.

Evie wondered if it was going to help or hurt their chances of catching him. Seeing his face flash across the screen she could tell the subtle differences between him and Anthony, but to the general public, they would look the same. She looked over at Anthony knowing it wasn't going to be easy for him. Everywhere he goes until this bastard is caught will mean he'll be questioned.

They all decided to stay on Noah's property for the day. They felt safe knowing the guards were all around. The men were still trying to find any other information they could about Jeremy, or Jay, or David and weren't coming up with much, which meant they were cranky. Even the Troublesome Trio were quiet. They all had their noses buried in books and would whisper quietly to each other every once in a while.

Evie watched Kat sit outside by herself most of the day. She seemed just to sit there and stare at nothing. Part of her wanted Kat to suffer, the other part of her wanted to help. She was about to go out to her when Lexi sat down with her. She didn't have to hear to know what they were talking about. Maybe they would be able to help each other, especially Lexi help Kat. Remembering the difference from Lexi before the first attack and right after, then how she healed and met Noah. Then another attack and more healing. Lexi could help her; she just had to be open to it.

Evie let the guys know that she was going back to the cottage to lie down. They hadn't been getting much sleep and all the time changes had done a number on her. She opened the windows and laid down letting the cool ocean breeze wash over her as she fell into a deep sleep.

~*~

Evie slowly came awake to the feel of someone's hands gently running up and down her body. For a brief moment she didn't know where she was or who could be touching her, but then she breathed in deep and smelled Anthony's scent.

"Good morning, la mia belezza. You missed dinner. I've brought it to you. Come, we'll eat on the balcony."

Evie stretched and got up. After freshening up she joined him. "Anything new after I left?"

Anthony shook his head. "No, and let's not talk about it. I just want a night away from it all. To just sit here and enjoy your company, look at your beautiful face and watch the stars come out."

That sounded wonderful to Evie. They spent a nice quiet evening just talking about their pasts and the hope for the future, with no mention of the darkness that was right outside their door.

Anthony stood and held his hand out to her. She could tell by the look in his eyes, it wasn't just to go to bed. With just the moonlight to guide them, he led them into the room and slowly started to undress her. "You look so beautiful in the moonlight. I could spend hours just looking at you." Using the back of his hand, his touch moved from her cheek, down her neck, across her nipple and down her stomach. Using his other hand he gripped the back of her neck and pulled her in for a deep kiss that made her weak in the knees.

Wanting to feel his skin she attempted to undress him while they kissed and his hand moved over her body knowing exactly where to touch for the most pleasure. Giving up she just ripped his shirt open by the buttons. They went from slow soft touches to a frenzy of tongues, touches and gripping each other. Their hands fumbling together trying to get his pants off. Finally, they were both naked, picking her up he thrust into her as they fell back on the bed.

She couldn't get him deep enough, she wanted to feel all of him, arching as much as she could it still wasn't enough. Forcefully, she rolled over so that she was on top of him, taking everything he had, riding him until they both collapsed in release.

~*~

Jeremy sat in a dirty rundown motel room wondering how his life had changed so much. They knew everything now. Every name he's ever used. The house he grew up in. His secret place where he kept his most precious pictures, his videos, his treasures. They were all gone now. He'd never see them again.

He felt like the little lost boy from so many years ago when his mother was willing to leave him with his asshole of a father. Having nowhere to turn, he was at a complete loss. Picking up a photo of Evie and Anthony he stared at it, trying to come up with some plan to make it all right again. *Maybe she was the key.* She seemed to make Anthony whole again, even after learning everything that had been done to him over the years. *Maybe she can make me whole again.* He put her photo down and picked up the cologne bottle knowing this was going to help him get close to her.

– CHAPTER TWENTY-ONE –

E vie woke up to the sun just starting to rise and an empty bed. Knowing she wasn't going to be able to sleep she got up and went downstairs to get some coffee Anthony had already brewed. She wondered where he was and when she went out on the back porch, she could see him standing at the water's edge. Taking a few gulps of coffee, she set the cup down on the railing and walked out to meet him. She stopped next to him and looked out over the ocean. The ocean was calm this morning, but she could see the clouds building quickly. Lexi's grandmother used to come out here every morning and Evie knew why now. It was so peaceful.

Sighing, when Anthony moved around to wrap his arms around her waist she tilted her head back breathing in his scent she loved so much. She ran her hands down his arms like she always did to lace her fingers with his and stopped. She started to struggle.

There was a scar. Looking down she saw the jagged width of it against the tan of his skin.

"I've got you now. I'm never letting go. I need you to change my luck," he hissed in her ear.

Her thoughts were whirling as he picked her up and started moving towards the ocean. It had gone from calm to thrashing waves in just a matter of seconds. She tried screaming but between the waves, wind and the lack of air in her lungs from him squeezing her so hard she barely got anything out.

"He can't have you. You're mine. You'll be my good luck charm. Everything is going to change now. I've got you."

"No, let me go." He had such a grip on her she couldn't move. She tried kicking him but couldn't get enough momentum to do any damage. Even when she did connect, it was like he didn't even feel it. Reaching back with one hand she tried to pull at his hair. He had it cut short so there was nothing for her to grab onto.

Reaching down she tried to pry back his fingers succeeding in breaking one of them before he squeezed her so hard she felt her ribs starting to break. Gasping for air as they got deeper and deeper into the water she knew her time was running out. Forcing her down under the water, she frantically searched the bottom of the ocean for anything that could become a weapon.

Her fingers glanced over rocks but not able to grab one before he turned her in the water. Feeling him against her, she could feel how hard he was and it made her sick. The burning in her lungs was getting worse. She knew she didn't have much longer. Trying to do anything she could, she made herself sink, hoping to either take him with her or get closer to the rocks.

Finally her hands found a rock pulling with all of her might it wouldn't budge. The ringing in her ears was getting louder and she knew she was going to have to take a breath soon, and then it would all be over.

Moving to the next rock she was able to get a grip on it and with every last bit of energy she swung as hard as she could at what she thought was his head. The last of her breath left her lungs as they floated away from each other into blackness.

~*~

Anthony was working in the downstairs office of the cottage when he heard Evie wake up and come downstairs, pour herself some coffee, then go out the backdoor. He wanted to finish this email before going out to join her on the beach. Since learning about Jeremy, he'd spent almost every waking hour wanting his revenge. It grew, almost completely taking him over. After hearing Kat's story, he knew what it could end up doing to him. Feeling like he was on the verge of something huge he paused. He thought he'd heard something.

Fear gripping him as he rushed out of the house and onto the beach to see Evie being pulled into the water. His knees almost buckled. Panic rushed headlong into him; there was nothing he could do to stop it. He knew he had to get ahold of himself. Racing towards the water, he could smell the rain in the air and the wind had picked up. The waves crashed harder on the beach. Pulling his phone from his pocket to call the main house, he heard footsteps running towards him. Looking over he saw security heading in his direction.

"No!" he screamed as he saw Jeremy holding Evie under the water for too long. Moving as fast as he could through the water, his only thought was getting to her. Saving her. It felt like a nightmare, where no matter how fast you move, you still aren't going anywhere and your destination just keeps getting further away.

Jeremy was so focused on Evie he didn't hear Anthony's scream. Anthony watched as an arm came up out of the water with a rock in it and hit the side of Jeremy's head. Jeremy fell into the water and started to float away. Anthony knew he had to get to Evie, she hadn't surfaced. With the waves beating at him, his only thought was of Evie. He couldn't find her. Time and time again he went under the water never finding her. Wanting to scream, rage and cry he knew they were running out of time. Finally his hand brushed against her. Taking her in his arms, he surfaced and started moving as fast as he could to shore never looking back to see what had become of Jeremy.

She was so cold and still in his arms. He fought back the thought that this could be the end. This vibrant woman, whom he'd spent so much time with was gone. He couldn't accept it. Lying her down, he started mouth-to-mouth, begging her with each breath to fight and start breathing. He almost started sobbing like a baby when she finally coughed up the seawater. Pounding on her back, he said a silent prayer when he heard the sirens approaching.

– CHAPTER TWENTY-TWO –

Images flashed through her mind. Jeremy. The water. No breath. Floating. Burning. Coughing. Anthony. Anthony. She had to get back to him. Slowly, she opened her eyes and there he was. Trying to lift her arm she found that she couldn't, frowning she tried to look around but couldn't take her eyes off of Anthony. Her rock. He was here. A tear escaped from her eye.

"Shhh… la mia belezza, everything is fine. You'll be okay. No, don't try to talk, you're safe. You're going to be okay."

"Jeremy?"

He reached over for the water and she took a sip, soothing her burning throat. "They're looking for his body. You scared the hell out of me. I went out to join you on the beach and he had you. A storm blew up quickly. All of a sudden, I heard people running in my direction. I knew I had to get to you, they wouldn't make it in time." He bowed his head. "I couldn't get to you fast enough. I saw everything. I thought he was going to kill you. Then you had the rock and swung it. I saw the blood burst from the side of his head and he floated away. My only thought was of you." He smoothed the hair back from her face. "All I thought about was getting to you. I pulled you from the water and we got most of it from your lungs. But you wouldn't wake up. I've never been so scared in my whole life. I couldn't lose you."

"I'm here," she whispered, "I'm not going anywhere."

He leaned over so that their foreheads were touching. "You'd better be. I can't see my life without you. Those few moments when I thought you were dead were the worst in my life. Worse than anything else Jeremy had done to me. I'd be lost in the storm without you."

"Sounds like you're stuck with me."

"Sounds like it. I love you, Evie. I don't know what the future holds. They are still looking for Jeremy's body. With the storm, the current made it difficult to search. I'm not going to rest until I know he won't hurt us anymore. But I can't live without you. If I have to choose, continuing my search for Jeremy running around the world or you, I choose you."

"Anthony, I love you. I know we can do this together. No matter what, we've seen the worst and now we can reach for the best, together."

They had been so wrapped up in each other they didn't notice Lexi and Noah at the doorway until Lexi started sniffling. Evie looked over at her and smiled. "Now, who's doing the ugly face cry?"

"Shut up." She raced to Evie's side and hugged her. "I'm so happy you're alive." Lexi looked at Anthony. "Thank you. Thank you for saving her." She leaned over and hugged him. Noah walked up behind her and put his hand on her back offering her his support.

Seeing the two people who meant so much to her embrace, Evie lost it and started crying. It was all going to be okay. *They* were all going to be okay.

– EPILOGUE –

Crawling up on the beach, Jeremy collapsed, gasping for breath. He had no idea where he was or what he was going to do next, but he was alive.

Rolling over on his back, he stared up at the blue sky. For the first time, he had to run. They were chasing him instead of him leading them around. Not liking that fact, he had to calm himself down, think things out logically so he didn't make any more mistakes.

THE END

CAUGHT IN THE STORM

Coming May 2014

Jackson Taylor spent his life doing what he wanted, when he wanted. But when the people he cares about the most start getting hurt, he decides it's time to come home for good and get involved in finding the person responsible. He wasn't anticipating finding something he'd lost years ago.

Kat Snyder had spent the past (fill in how many years) years hiding from everyone and blending into the background while she searched for the man who destroyed her. Bent on returning the favor, she pushed everything and everyone aside on her quest for revenge.

Will Jackson come through when he's most needed? Will Kat learn to grow and trust again? Find out when they get Caught in the Storm.

Coming August 1, 2014

The Moonlight Cravings Anthology
Nine paranormal tales… one HOT night.

DREAMING IN MOONLIGHT – M. STRATTON, MOONLIGHT THUNDER – SCARLETT DAWN, **HEXED BY MOONLIGHT - GENA D. LUTZ,** MOONLIGHT POSSESSIONS - KELLEE GILMORE, **RAPTURE BY MOONLIGHT - JACQUIE UNDERDOWN,** MOONLIGHT RHAPSODY – LAURA THALASSA, **SPELLBOUND IN MOONLIGHT - S. E. GILCHRIST,** MOONLIGHT MASTER - MORGAN JANE MITCHELL, **MOONLIGHT DANCE - JESSICA CAGE**

DREAMING IN MOONLIGHT

Ghosts are real. They are all around us. Most of the time they are satisfied to watch us go by and not interact. When a couple was cursed to spend three hundred years in death searching for the one living couple that could release their bonds they look for centuries to find a love that will make time stand still.

If they fail they will be sent to Hell to live out the rest of eternity.

Demons are real. They are all around us. Their one goal is make our lives a living hell. They will stop at nothing to destroy our minds and bodies. With the curse rapidly approaching its end the deepest darkest demon is summoned to make sure they don't succeed.

Kate O'Malley fell in love with the old two story farm house in Maine at first sight. She had to live there. Spending all of her savings she was able to buy it and moved right in. The very first night strange things happened. Her dreams aren't her own. Looking for answers she calls on a friend who puts her in contact with a ghost hunter, Sawyer Hamilton. Neither knew what was in their future, neither knows if they are going to survive it.

Dreaming in Moonlight when your sleep is filled with passion and your nightmares are real.

Made in the USA
Charleston, SC
01 April 2015